UNBELONGING

Gayatri Sethi

Mango & Marigold Press

Beloved reader,

I write these words during a global pandemic as fascism rises around the world. We are living through the largest protests in human history while enduring unprecedented oppressions. Many of us feel deeply disconnected from our communities and increasingly isolated.

Why is this a book about unbelonging?

At a time when weaponization of identity fuels wars and xenophobia ends too many lives, I am all the more cognizant that belonging is a core human need.

Rachel Ricketts   *Our deepest need as humxns is belonging, so feeling constantly othered, ostracized, and unwanted, especially as a result of speaking truth to your own oppression, is incredibly painful.*

I am intimately familiar with the kinds of real, tangible, mental, emotional, and even spiritual harms that result from unbelonging. I wrote this book to offer open-hearted explorations of the kinds of emotional violence enacted by laws and policies that marginalize folks like me.

I drafted this book during the 2016-2020 Trump era.
I revised it during a year of social isolation imposed by Covid-19.
I could not have written this book out of my trauma alone. I have been on an intentional and vigilant journey to heal myself from the pain of unbelonging. This journey is ongoing. There are many truths and lessons that remain unspoken.
One day, this book about how identity, oppression, and

colonialism have impacted my personhood and life will no longer be relevant. I dream that this book, and its theme of unbelonging, will be obsolete. For now, I feel moved to offer these pages in as raw and true a form as I can muster.

Don't we have a moral responsibility to each other to learn, grow, and dismantle oppression within and around us?

This book is for all of us struggling to process our sense of self and belonging in our families, relationships, communities, and world at large. We may be the others, the margin dwellers, the oft overlooked and rarely fully valued. We may have all the answers but need more questions. We may have a vague sense there is more to learn about ourselves and are seeking a place from which to begin.

Though the world we live in does not embrace or celebrate us, I wish that you might see glimmers of new possibilities for being and unbelonging.

Thank you for reading bravely with an open heart and mind.

In solidarity,
Gayatri

Contents

Foreword   11

Reader's Guide   13

Introductions: Who Am I?   17

DESI·*ish*   27

AFRICAN·*ish*   81

AMERICAN·*ish*   133

    i. Revelations   135

    ii. Conversations   161

    iii. Revolutions   223

ACTIVE MEDITATIONS   267

Appendix   283

    i. Create Your Own Glossary   284

    ii. Citations   289

    iii. Create Your Own Reading List   290

    iiii. Gratitudes and Acknowledgements   292

Foreword

James Baldwin   *The place where we belong does not exist.*
We will build it.

I am a perpetual migrant. I am an unsettled and unsettling person. I come from a line of peoples who were either forcibly removed from their homes or immigrated across borders built by colonial violence. Migrant stories like mine are full of gaps and gasps. They do not lend themselves easily to linearity or conventional form. Sometimes, the words "migrant" and "immigrant" themselves assume a stability in origin and residence that many of us do not experience.

There are no sonnets or villanelles here. There are many cathartic possibilities in writing in free verse. I often write in free form because questions related to identity and belonging defy form and format. Essays require a kind of certitude that I have not been able to muster. What I offer in this collection are reflections, invocations, and verses. This is not a life story with beginnings and endings. Rather, I write between genres to open up windows into my unbelonging.

What is it like to be multiply othered in today's world, rife with xenophobia? I exhale in the form of open-ended reflections. Many of these pages read like laments. The emotional landscapes of unbelonging are laid open. There is a deliberate messiness in these pages. How can a disrupted and flawed human write in perfect form? If you read in between the lines, you might also find hope, persistence, and resilience.

If some of these verses appear didactic, this is authentic to my identity. I am an educator and teacher at heart. I spent many years offering lessons and designing curricula in college classrooms. Some pages might feel like lecture notes. Others might require further research to fully understand.

I offer you my words with an earnest and open heart.

I use words in multiple tongues and make cultural references without italics, footnotes, or explanations. This, too, is an intentional choice. I live as a translated human. I am always translating myself for others. Perhaps, in exerting effort to decipher these references, we might grasp what this act of translation means for "others" like me.

This collection embraces unbelonging.

Reader's Guide

A FEW SUGGESTIONS AS YOU READ THIS BOOK

This book is intended to be an interactive, brave space of reflection, healing, and creation. Many holistic educators believe that learning is healing. True learning shifts us from discomfort to understanding by engaging our heads, hearts, and hands.

ENGAGE

The words and illustrations herein are created to evoke a warm embrace even as you might feel new emotions and be challenged by some of these uncomfortable truths. It is my earnest hope that you will experience this book with both your mind and body. Highlight words. **Doodle in the margins. Scratch out words.** Fold the pages if you are so inclined. Add your own ideas. Write your own reflections in the margins or blank spaces. Express yourself!

REFLECT

Use the prompts and inquiries to self-reflect. Create space to process your own observations and experiences related to these themes. Passive reading does not result in shifts in understanding.

CLAIM YOUR OWN LEARNING

When you encounter a new word or phrase, circle it and add it to the self-created glossary pages at the end of the book. Engage with the concepts highlighted in the invitations to research. There are fields of study and well-known authors and researchers whose scholarship informed this work. They are cited throughout. Create your own reading list based on what you read here.

SHARE

This book is designed to be a multifaceted reading experience–equal parts poetry collection, workbook, and journal. If these words, verses, and inquiries provoke new understandings or creativity, feel free to create your own art in these pages and outside them. Start a conversation. Share the book's ideas with your circle of friends and community. Start a book club. Create new possibilities.

Content warnings

Systemic racism

Anti-Blackness

Partition trauma

Abuse

Interpersonal violence

Xenophobia

Immigrant trauma

Casteism

Misogyny

Anxiety

INTRODUCTIONS

Why Identify?

Identity matters.
We see color.
We are not invisible.
We are not ether.

Race is a construction
and race has real life ramifications.

Name all the intersections.
If we do not say who we are,
if we do not claim all our selves,
we will be erased.

We need to see how we are differently placed
before we can claim to all be one human race.

Identify.

Identity

Who I am is always in flux.
Keeping up with who I am and who I become has always been
my quest.
Who am I?

In my moments of clarity, I remember.
In my moments of angst and despair, I don't quite know.

My identity has been policed.
All my life somebody has tried to tell me who I'm not.

You're not Indian.
Your Hindi sounds foreign, like childish talk.
You're not Tanzanian.
Your Kiswahili and birth certificate don't prove you belong here.
Lekgoa, they call me in Botswana.

Lekgoa?

But, I am not the white person who has money.
We are humble and brown.
Aren't we?

Futsek. Go back to where you came from.
Where is that exactly?

I came to america.
Naively thinking I'd find myself here.
They asked me, "what are you?"
Neither black nor white.

Neither here nor there.

Claim my Indian self?
The desis mocked my "African" and western ways.

"I wasn't raised in India," I said.
"But I do speak Hindi and understand Punjabi and Gujarati.
My extended family still lives there.
I used to visit."

Eye roll. Dismissed.

But they're right.
I defied the Indian ways.
I didn't want to be a subservient girl who passively accepted
roles assigned to her.
I despised caste discrimination.
Classism and anti-Blackness made me rage.
Arranged marriage? No, thanks.

Who am I?

I'm the one who proves I can. I'll defy. I resist.
I've always had this fire in me.
I married who I loved.
I defied the boundaries. Knowing more walls and separations
would come from this choice.

"He's African american. That's just not done. No Indian girl
ought to shame her community that way."

Wait a minute.

You police me, but say I am not desi enough.
The desi card was never mine. So why fuss now?
What business of yours is it who I marry or why?

We disown you. We block you. We stonewall you.
Indian? I wasn't born in India.
I'm not African. I was born there.
I'm not american though I sometimes speak and act like I am.
My children are (Indian)-African-american.

We are punctuated with hyphens and parentheses.
I'm not sure what goes before or after my hyphens.
Some parts of me remain hidden in parentheses. (Bahá'í)

Who am I?

I'm a hyphenated human.
I'm adept at adapting where I go.
I'm a polyglot.
Malleable.
I speak many tongues.
I have numerous personas.
Survival.
I make myself at home, but I'm not sure where I belong.
Some days, my hyphens and parentheses erase me.
For all of this, I'm judged.
I'm judged harshly for being inauthentic. Fake. Condescending.
Too much this. Not enough that.
Do you judge me because you don't understand me?

Identity. Who am I?

All I know is
you don't decide who I am.

I do.

Struggle Song

Where do I belong?
Where on earth do I belong?

UnBox Me

We are expected to check boxes
but who lives in boxes?
This or that?
Here or there?
Pick one box.
Check it.

I am other.
I am also all of the above.
Am I everything?

A wise poet oft quoted says,
I contain multitudes.
Truer words I never heard
said about myself.
We cannot be contained
in boxes or closets or binaries.

Humans are fluid.
I flow in the gaps.
I live in the intersections.
I live in the margins.
I even inhabit the margins of the intersections.

I cannot be divided or carved up into sections.
I cannot check a box.

I would be split
on the atomic level
and then everything else,
like the box,
would explode.

Around the globe,
hate crimes are proliferating.
Politicians threaten to "send us back."
People demand, "Go back to where you came from."

Send me back?

Beware if you attempt to "send me back"
you will have to piece me up.
Partition me. Into multitudes.
Send my head in parts to all the lands and places

where I've lived and learned.

But how much of my head will you keep here
in this land called america?
As I have studied and labored and taught at places of higher
learning built on the land whose original keepers are the Yurok,
Muscogee, and Illini.

Send my heart to the Lake Victoria region of Tanzania where I
was born.
Send my hands to the land that is now known as Pakistan where
my ancestors were born two generations ago.
Send my insides to India, Punjab—
where my people have resided after Partition.

Send an organ of your choosing to Iran,
the birthplace of the faith I follow.

They might return it to the sender.

Beware if you try to send me back you must send me
to Botswana where I was raised,
where my passport says I am a citizen.

Send my feet to all the lands and places
 I've traveled and sojourned-
too many to name from Aruba to Cuba to France to Mauritius to
Trinidad to Zimbabwe.

Won't you please send tiny pieces of me
to everywhere I've felt at home
and at peace?
The Caribbean and Mediterranean Seas.
The Indian and Atlantic Oceans.

Keep my uterus in america
because it held and birthed
american children.
This land is rightfully theirs—despite all the denial—
as their paternal people are descended from those enslaved by
this land's settlers.

Their ancestors built this land.
They were raised to respect this land.

If I leave my american children here—the most precious parts of me—
I dread and fear
you will discard or exile them, too,
as you disown their immigrant parent.

Perhaps, I will take my progeny with me
to lands still unknown where we will know no fear
because of
the colors of our skin
our worship practices
our names.

Beware if you attempt to send me back,

partition me piece by piece,
too many pieces, traces of me
will be left behind in america's soil.

How will you erase or recompense me
for the cumulative impact of my existence here?

As my soul is indivisible,
she will roam unshackled and borderless wherever she pleases
to be.
Send me back?
Piece by piece, yet
I will remain intact.

Symptoms of Unbelonging: A self-diagnosis

Longing Discomfort Sabotage Malaise Insecurity Anxiety
Mania Paranoia Wanderlust Fernweh Meraki Eunoia
Ataraxia Hodophilia Be/longing

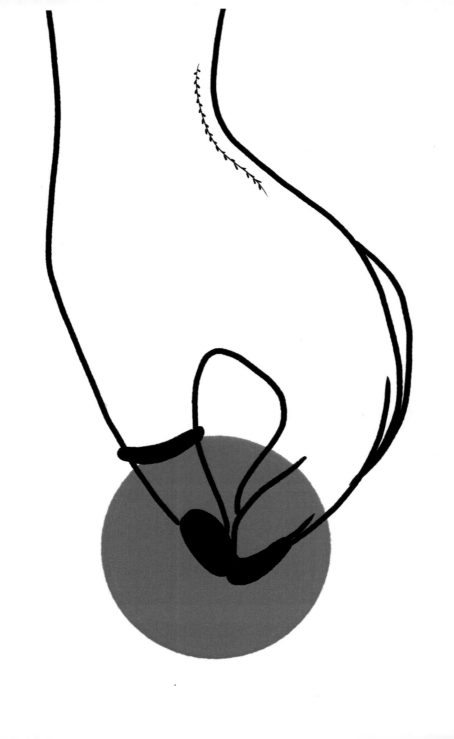

DESI·ish

i am desi-ish
because i do not have any other words to convey
the complex diasporic perpetual immigration
unbelonging
story that unravels in me and around me.

i say i am desi-ish because
although i trace my lineage to punjab,
i was not born or raised there.
my mother pined for her desh
with the deep patriotic longing
that i acknowledge in her
without feeling myself.
to be born away from the desh
is to speak its tongues,
understand its words,
and still seek meaning.
it is to seek your heritage,
love your origins,
while resisting imposed parameters
of belonging.

what does it mean to be desi-ish?
it is to ever know but not know.
it is to belong but defy.
it is to understand but resist.

mantra deity

i was blessed with a distinctly desi name.
gayatri.
gayatri is a mantra.
it is sacred.
gayatri is a deity.
she is the embodiment
of transcendent knowledge.
she represents the knowing that
defies rationality
and invites spirituality.

i do not fully understand how i am,
brown child born on african soil,
to a father who relinquished his hindu identity
to embrace a faith associated with islam by his hindu kin.

how did my parent who did not press his
palms together, but rather invoked allah
palms open to the heavens,
name me after a hindu deity
and a mantra
he rarely invoked or chanted?

this is the conundrum of my name,
and so it rarely conveys my own sense of me.

i do know that my mother
prayed this mantra like it was a lifeline,
and still does.

it is her name with invocations
for me.

will i ever live in or up to my name?

to be desi-ish is to know that names matter.
naming and self-naming are powerful.

brown folks' mantras | मंत्र

what are the mantras of brown girls
in distress?

our goddesses are bold, stunning, and fierce:
saraswati, knowledge and art
lakshmi, wealth and prosperity
parvati, the divine mother.

by other names, they are:
durga, the fiercest form of the divine mother

kali, the keeper of time and life. death, too.

let us invoke them!

what are their mantras?
be you.
be fierce.
be fiery.
be a force.

our mantras are life giving.
let us chant them!

what are the chants of those
who have no mantras, no deities?

i do not know.
this is a conundrum,
i know.

ask the ancestors?
invoke the ancestors.

Frantz Fanon   *in the world through which i travel, i am endlessly*
creating myself.

words they call me
those who know me call me: mama aunty bua teacher professor masi friend mentor scholar sister dada fam kin beti didi bibi

gayatri

they say: you are honest a truth-teller fearless safe kind protector knower insightful wise fierce a revolutionary one of us.

words matter. names matter.

those who look at me but do not know me throw
around these words:
immigrant

other   **migrant**

brown

woman of color

bipoc   **south asian**

desi

opinionated

proud

condescending   threatening

outspoken

confusing   crazy   woke

articulate   angry   defiant

radical

exotic

foreign   divisive

disruptive

disgraceful

do they see me?
do they even know me?

thank heavens i know myself
enough to
not be limited
constrained
or contained
by words that are not
my own.

names matter. words matter.

naming is healing

for those of us who are wounded by weaponized unbelonging
even by those who share identities with us,
there is a deep healing power in learning to name and identify
ourselves.

Boli | ਬੋਲੀ

our poetry is spoken word.
you hear us not.
we write here.
you see us not.
we right here.
you feel us not.
boliyaan.
our spoken word is spoken word.

are you?

are you indian? no.
are you south asian? sort of.
are you south asian american? not quite.
are you asian? depends.
are you indo-african? maybe.
are you desi? desi-ish.

ish

i say i am "ish" when speaking about my identities. i belong and unbelong.
there are many of us all over the globe who are "ish" people.

our struggles and pain, as well as joys and victories, are a part of us.

there is healing in learning new words and concepts to name our experiences.

many wise folks say that naming is a key to healing.

Audre Lorde   *if i did not define myself for myself, i would be crunched into other people's fantasies for me and eaten alive.*

Janet Mock   *there is a power in naming yourself, in proclaiming to the world that this is who you are.*

to be desi-ish is to know that chai
is sacred.
if you decline chai, you might not be desi at all.

why chai why

chai
i'm exhausted
chai pilo
my heart aches
chai piyo
i'm feeling so moody, yaar
chalo, chai piyen
i'm lonely

drink your chai
why?

joy, celebration, or festivity
sorrow, grief, or mourning
it is chai time.

we desi folks
do not speak openly of our emotions
we rarely are real about our feelings
mental illness is taboo.

so what do we do?
chai
we sip so much chai.

chai is the cure-all for
the ailing heart and soul.

our perpetual
chai ki chyas
is a bottomless thirst
insatiable
with each cup of chai
we swallow our feelings
yearning for healing.

why?
who needs therapy?
boil your milk and tea leaves
stir stir stir in the secret masala
sweeten
boil and boil and boil
strain out the stresses and worries
sit sip exhale

repeat
why chai
chai is the hope for healing
chai is the mysterious cure
for all the angst
that will not be
spoken or expressed.

chai on repeat.
why chai?
don't ask,
just sip sip sip.

do not ask why
you still feel empty.

there is fleeting chai-n चाय
in chai.

maybe we chant
chai-n
lips whispering prayer
as we sip.

> ***to be desi-ish***
> ***is to decline***
> ***the mithai.***
> ***what heresy.***

death by gulaab jamun

let me tell you a horror story
of an aunty
who was allergic
to dairy
gluten
nuts shuts too.
hay haye
thoo thoo
who's ever heard
of such a curse?

what kind of goree cursed
this aunty?
she can't even eat
mithai
or sip chai.
what kind of living hell
is this kala jadoo?
can you imagine
never ever tasting
a paratha dripping with ghee?
no paneer bhajee?
can you imagine saying
"nah thank you"
when the ladoos shadoos
are passed around?
drinking earl grey or darjeeling
or assam with no sugar
and calling it tea?
what curse is this for a desi
to be condemned to death
by gulaab jamun
because she is allergic to
goddess only knows what?

we don't believe in allergies
we would just
say our mantra shantra
eat the damn
gulaab jamun.

to be desi-ish
is to understand that
pressure is often confused for love.

punjabi beti | बेटी

i am the first-born beti
to a first-born beta
first granddaughter poti
in a family of punjabi
refugees torn apart
by partition.

what pressures compress
my brown girl body
in the name of duty or loyalty
to community?

लोग and दुनिया | ਲੋਕ and ਦੁਨੀਆ

punjab existed before india.
punjab existed before pakistan.
punjab existed before the raj.
punjab is the land of my ancestors.

root truth

the more i water the roots of my heritage, the more i grow into myself.

when i claim my roots and adore my multidimensional heritage i grow wings.

imperialism and colonialism

those of us with roots in the south asian continent were colonial subjects. imperialism and colonialism are processes of occupation and domination. colonial forces took over, ruled, and partitioned the lands of my ancestors. imperial forces continue to suppress our heritage and dominate our ideas, behaviors, minds, bodies, and spirits. when we speak of desi-ish postcolonial identity and heritage, colonialism and imperialism must be named and confronted as defining realities. we speak of both in past tense but they are omnipresent.

RESEARCH:
Forms of Colonialism
Colonialism v. Imperialism
Decolonization

to be desi-ish
is to be too westernized, by desi standards,
to practice the traditions
we desi-ish question
and subvert.

my desi-ish ways are disruptive
and have had me reprimanded.
i am called a "disgraceful desi."
like the *feminist killjoy,*
the disgraceful desi might reclaim her title
to turn the injury into an honor.

Sara Ahmed

head cover, sir dhak lo

i confess i loathed the elders' reminders to
cover my head.

i used to wonder about the aunties
stirring daal with their chunnis
wrapped around their heads.
i would judge them harshly
for their old timey ways.

liberate yourselves!
shed your head coverage
shed the patriarchal bondage.

we don't need to cover ourselves.
we can be free.

let go of the veils and dupattas!
let go of the old ways,
i found myself thinking.
you wouldn't find me anywhere
with a scarf on my head or
a shawl over my shoulders.

i needed to feel free
even with kin and community,
as an educated person rarely conforming to tradition,
i could not appear *other*.

Chandra
Mohanty

imagine my surprise
to find that these days,
i've been head covering
without consciously realizing it,

like my ancestral women,
wearing dupattas of ivory or saffron or gold.

these head coverings
bring me safety, comfort, and solace.

it's as if the ancestral spirits
have removed a veil from my heart
whispered a truth to my soul.
true freedom comes

not from giving up our traditions
but from embracing our own authentic ways.

sir dhak lo.
cover my head.

to be a desi-ish
who head covers selectively
like the bibis in punjab
is to revoke the number white feminism does on me.

my she/her/hers are pronounced
in desi life as an endless
list of rules
regulations
requirements.

mantras for enoughness

i affirm
i am a work in progress.
i am enough,
i am more than enough.
it is unbelievable how enough i am.

to be desi-ish is to be both
constrained and privileged by model minority myths.
it is to be both the oppressed and the oppressor.

what anti-Blackness looks like

when we are neither
Black nor
white
when we are benefitting from
proximity
to whiteness
or when we fleetingly
feign allegiance with other folks of color

when we are discreetly
anti-Black while
claiming to be "people of color"

but maybe we feel shame about being oppressed
so we ally with whiteness

we shy away from our Black kin
ignoring our collective humanity

we minimize their pain
while claiming to be discriminated against
all the while choosing
to drown in whiteness

48

denying our pigmentation
justifying gentrification

we who are overly invested
in being the exceptions
we seek to shine as "model minorities"
we are messengers of the master's rules
claiming we all must pull ourselves up by our
boot
straps

but we are the master's fools
with our boots on the throats of
our Black kin
to climb up the master's ladder
and in climbing claim
that our brethren's lives don't matter

we are complicit in adding insult injury and harm

we the brown
the neither here
nor there

we the brown
we must shift this tide
instead of drowning ourselves in whiteness
to obfuscate our pigmentation

we could turn the tide
we could step off the throats of Black folks
and kneel bend tend with

UNBELONGING

deep bows of our backs

not to the masters as their fools
but in solidarity with Black folks

knowing and living the truth
that any gain we claim
at their expense
is only pain

pain pain pain
we all fall
we all drown
could we just know this without a doubt

no lives nor gains nor climbs matter
unless and until Black lives matter.

Audre Lorde *for the master's tools will never dismantle the master's house.
they may allow us temporarily to beat him at his own game, but
they will never enable us to bring about genuine change.*

*to be desi-ish is to edit, to correct ourselves when we write
capital-d desi and lowercase-b Black.*

who taught me to hate myself?
who taught me to love myself?

to be desi-ish
is to hold privileges while being intimate
with oppression.

what happens at the intersections
of faith

class

caste

when we enjoy
privilege of one kind
while being oppressed
by our own kind?

---

about me

it is paternal family history (or perhaps fantasy) that we are descendents of
kashyap rishi. this possibly places some of my ancestors in kashmir.
it is maternal family history (not quite fantasy) that my nani was a freedom
fighter. even in 1945, as an educated young woman, child of a law professor,
she fought colonial powers and served time in jail. the elders who knew her say
i remind them of her.

the sethi family relocated to delhi from rawalpindi.
the chaudhry family fled to chandigarh via shimla from lahore.

nani passed away in childbirth in 1947. my mother was a year old. although the twins my nani birthed, my uncles, survived for a few months, they passed away in refugee camps when my family fled from lahore to shimla. these collective losses have shaped our family stories in ways i am still discovering.

nanaji was an attorney. the story i heard was that his muslim friend and colleague smuggled his law library to him from lahore and he began his life anew. he might have been the first mayor of shimla post-partition. he wore only desi cotton. he burned his western clothing and resisted colonial rule. he served in the high court of punjab. he rarely smiled. he raised his six surviving children without remarrying. his sister, estranged from her family arrangements, lived in the family home.

my father contracted polio at age one. he had a lifelong disability from this childhood illness. my mother contracted typhoid and suffered an extended childhood illness that resulted in the right side of her body being paralyzed.

in the mid 1960's, my father, the eldest son of the family, converted from the arya samaaj hinduism of his parents to espouse the Bahá'í faith. this choice cemented our unbelonging to family, relations, culture, and even caste.

this unconventional decision led him to leave his home and biological family to journey alone to east africa where he was a secondary school teacher in a remote town in tanzania.

my parents' partnership was arranged. my father returned to new delhi briefly for the wedding. my mother, who had led a relatively sheltered existence in chandigarh, accompanied him to rural tanzania where i was born a year and a half later.

RESEARCH:

Sikh Empire

Indentured labor from South
Asia

1947 Partition

to be desi-ish is to be only thirteen
and already burdened with expectations around marriage.

a note to my aunties from my younger self

dear desi aunties and mamis,
real talk. sach bolo.
you are raising your children on a steady diet
of toxic masculinity and patriarchal abuse.

what is all this rishta obsession?
what if you didn't force your daughters to marry?
what if you didn't tell your twelve-year-olds that marriage
defines their purpose?

what if you stopped matchmaking?
what if you stopped all this shaadi marriage frenzy?

you say you do this because you love us.

love isn't control.
love isn't authority.
love isn't fearful.
love doesn't shame.
love doesn't threaten or require obedience.

you control and patronize us in the name of love.

let us call it what it is: this is abuse.
what if you let your daughter just be?

let us daughters breathe?
let us find our own way?
let us love and be loved how we choose?

let me ask you:
how has marriage suited you?
how was your rishta?
were you shackled into servitude?
while secretly wishing for your paint brushes or sitar?

did you find your joy?
did you hide your poetry, stop reading for pleasure, and forget
your profession?
were you secretly seething, abused by the in-laws?
did the uncles' moods rule every day?

did you cry silent suffering into your pillow many a night?
did you consider ending your life or running away to free
yourself?
damn the married life, and fantasize about your escape?

did you succumb and become numb to the abuse and think this
was "normal"?

abuse is not normal is not love.
love does not control.
love does not shame.
love does not demand obedience.
love does not justify silence.

and here you are, repeating the cycles of abuse with your
children.

you dare arrange their rishtas, fates, and futures
to set them up
for exploitation and abuse?

why not set those daughters free of
expectations
constrictions
control
fear
shame?

why not raise them to
create
build
imagine
their own life and love
with or without
marriage?

to be desi-ish
is to live under
patriarchal cultural norms
even as i rage defiantly
within.

who taught me to hate myself?

the patriarchy taught me to hate myself. compulsory
heterosexist marriage obsession is hateful. we are taught that,
born female, we have no value or worth outside of patriarchal
parameters.

colorism taught me lies about myself. classism taught me i was
labor.

under the guise of good intentions, aunties and strict teachers
who uttered words of colorism, casteism, and classism put me
in my place. i came to doubt my worth. i learned early in life that
the world does not value little brown girls with modest financial
means residing on african soil.

i was fourteen when an elder
informed me that i was not to marry a Black person
even though i lived in africa.
we are indians and indians marry their own kind.

disgraceful desi

what could a desi daughter possibly do to be condemned
as a disgrace?

he was Black.
he had been married before.
he was muslim.
he had a ten-year-old son.

log kya kahenge? what will society say?
this tight rope that binds desi daughters to tradition.

i transgressed.
i defied.

i became a disgrace
by marrying my beloved.

log are still talking about it.
it has been twenty years and counting
since i became a disgraceful desi daughter.

to be desi-ish
is to chuckle with recognition
because log kya kahenge
is desi code that desis understand.

my brown desi indian self

i had a dream in which someone asked me "what's up with you
and india?"
i replied that i'm one of her alienated daughters seeking
reconciliation.

i haven't visited since i was eighteen.
my pa bought me a ticket and sent me solo as a precondition to
going to college in the u.s.
he predicted i wouldn't go on my own.
he had a way of just knowing. memories are fleeting.

i cherish the conversations i had with my mataji while shelling
peas, marveling at her slow and gentle ways. i chuckle at the
shenanigans with my cousins. i smile thinking of the meals with
buas and uncles, forty or more of us talking and eating all at
once in one tight space.

growing up on another continent, we didn't have such festivity.
we didn't have history together like this. we didn't quite fit. we
spoke hindi and heard punjabi (how we managed this while
growing up on african soil is a feat unto itself), but our accents
made everyone laugh.

we were teased for being firangi.

my father wasn't a patriotic person. he wore his indian-ness with detachment. his heart was at home in africa and he wished to rest there.

i am his child after all.

i recall feeling like an insider and outsider all at once in india. i have physical recollections of the discomfort, the clenching of my muscles.

i have not been back.

i know that there's reconciliation to be done. but, i'm keenly aware of the shadows there that make me weep.
my people do not look kindly upon me being vocal about my pain. they hush me up and reprimand me often for what i do say. let us remember that our desi cultures do not take kindly to bold "outspoken" women.

let me recall where i have been raised and lived.

i hide my desi. i do not deny it even as i defy it.
i call upon my ancestors often.

i work on owning myself while keeping my distance.

who taught me to doubt myself?
who taught me to value myself?

***to be desi-ish is
to be uprooted and replanted
so often that
one sprouts wings from the unearthed roots.***

every human in every hue who policed my identity taught me to doubt myself. if i was not this enough, i was not that enough, either. for a child learning they are neither here nor there, seeds of self-doubt sprout into stems that split in the wind. every gust blows them over and strips them of their fragile leaves. unable to stand, they droop until they know not who nor what they are. i was a brittle-stemmed human seeking the sunlight for much of my life.

***i am desi-ish
because as i go about living my life
code switching as i do,
brown desi men
often mistake me for a non-desi
and even when i speak in hindi or punjabi,
they question me repeatedly to verify my desi-worthiness.***

shades of brown

i dwell in shades
of brown.

i swell with
melanation
and take joy in my coloration.

*to be desi-ish is to often be unaware
of one's true history and ancestry.*

partition–we are kin
on the 14th of august, 1947 pakistan was born.
on the 15th of august, 1947 india was "independent."
the british called it transfer of power.
the indians called it independence day.

it was partition day.

one and a half million lives were lost.
among them, my maternal grandmother.
1% of the world's people became refugees.
my ancestors were uprooted from their punjab and fled across
a random border to the other side. they left everything.

partition.

they never went back.
none of us have ever returned.

we carry the traumas of uprooting as soul wounds.
passed down generation to generation.

we bear the soul scars of severance from homelands.

partition.

we are in parts, separated from each other.
we do not recall that we are the same people.
we the pakistani, we the hindustani, we the bangladeshi.
we the muslim, we the sikh, we the hindu.

we are kin.
we do not remember.

74+ years.

i remember.
are we free yet?

**to be desi-ish
means to not hold any
national pride in india
but rather claim
sovereignty for kashmir as i declare
kinship with pakistan.**

घबराहट

this is the word in my mother's tongue
that signifies anxiety intermixed with paralyzing fear.
when i write what i write
about desi islamophobia,
my desi kin
are struck with paralyzing fear.
they try to silence me.

my words, they fear,
will have me attacked, exiled, or worse.
they fear for my safety
that my words calling out
hindu supremacy and fascism
will be the end of me.

ghubrahat.

their fears are not far-fetched.
their ghubrahat is not imagined.
read the news coming out of india.
patriarchal hindutva supremacy is the ruling party.

there are no words adequate to convey that ghubrahat.

we cannot chup karo
or else that will be the end.

हौसला

How do I quell my anxieties?

Who offers me comfort hosla in traumatizing times?

i am desi-ish
because when i recently traveled to the desh,
i was required to apply for a visa.
claiming kin in pakistan would have had this visa entry
declined.

i left out a few details.

we are at war with our kin.
partition is now.

we speak of 1947 as if it were the past
but partition rages on in us and around us.

it festers in the rampant islamophobia among hindus.
islamophobia is the disease my kin contracted in partition.

we carry and pass on the traumas of uprooting as soul wounds
of hate planted and exploited in us by colonizers,
passed down generation to generation.

we bear the soul scars of severance from truth.

in beforetimes, muslims and hindus and sikhs were bound in
oneness.

partition is not over.

we still wage war with ourselves.

Gayatri Sethi

***to be a desi-ish punjabi grandchild of partition
is to carry intergenerational transferred trauma.***

Tabitha
Mpamira-Kaguri

i have heard it said that unless trauma is
transformed, it is transferred.
this truth resonates tragically within me.

Kashmiri poet
I cannot drink water
It is mingled with the blood of young men who have died up in the mountains.
I cannot look at the sky
It is no longer blue; but painted red.

---

seeing red for kashmir

i'm seeing red for kashmir.
our tricolor flags are waving
in hues of red.

why are we not mourning?

after 74+ years of partition,
the flag-waving patriots
are warmongering, bloodthirsty,
proclaiming hindu supremacy.

india, the democracy, is no more.
   we, the colonized,
   became colonizers.

have we counted the dead?
   do we see red?
do we bleed red?

i do not go to temple,
but i surely pray
we be healed from ingesting this
poison
of toxic patriarchy
and blind patriotism
that boil together to make us fascist
occupiers
who wave flags to display
our own freedoms
even as we defile and destroy
the freedoms of our kin.

i'm seeing red for kashmir.
i'm seeing red for india.

the democracy is a farce
we are now occupiers
we, the colonized,
   became colonizers.

let us wave the red-stained
flag at half mast.

i saw red for kashmir long before i was told by relatives that we have ancestry in this land. i am rarely surprised when i learn facts that confirm my feelings.

i remind myself that life is a sort of remembering.

i am named gayatri. i am the one who knows without knowing.

kisaan protest

i bear witness. the largest protest in human history originated in the lands of my ancestors. i witness thousands of bibis, youth, and kin protest throughout a pandemic to demand their haqq and declare kisaan majdoor zindaabad. in their chardi kala, fearless words, and steadfast actions, i recognize both trauma and lion courage.

i recognize in their eyes the kind of steely determination of my elders when they stood fast in their protest despite assaults on their dignity and humanity. whether it is the mard log dispensing the unfair blows or the fascist government, the womenfolk persist.

i bear witness. the months-long farmers' protests from punjab to delhi unlock a new understanding of punjabi loyalty to land and livelihood. even if we cannot join the frontlines, does it not behoove us to witness and resist, too?

who taught me to own myself?
who taught me to name myself?

speaking in tongues

i learned to speak in many tongues. --- kiswahili. --- --- --- english. --- punjabi. --- french. --- i would even speak hindi and write in the sanskrit alphabet. as an adult, i no longer recall how. i hear --- gujarati, --- spanish, --- setswana, and --- farsi, too. those who taught me words, names, concepts, ideas, and gave me a pencil so that i may ideate taught me to know myself. even as they did, they graded my assignments and wondered why i would not obey. i was a gifted student punished for talking too much. the teachers who taught me words but silenced my thoughts were many. the forces to silence brown children under the guise of making them polite and respectful were strong. these forces both shaped me and denied me.

i learned as an adult to reclaim my voice and my words. what i write and how i write are forms of self-claiming. i *speak in tongues*.

Chandra
Mohanty

i stitch the fractured and erased parts of myself back together into healing cohesion. i speak myself in multiple tongues.

lessons in obedience

we memorized our lessons.

we learned by rote memorization. we recited our knowledge word for word from the textbooks sent from india to the high commission in tanzania. we learned sanskrit and sang the anthem of a faraway land. we wore uniforms and we marched in straight lines. we sat in neat rows. we kept our silence. we raised our hands. we did not speak out of turn. we spoke when we were spoken to. we obeyed. we followed the rules. we deferred to our teachers. we were commanded to respect our elders.

we memorized our lessons.

we memorized obedience.

chup kar | चुप कर

dear culturally maladjusted disrupters who've been silenced by society, family, and community—
keep on speaking.

keep on raising the issues.

i'm the desi annoying and embarrassing her people by talking openly about all the taboo topics.

queerness: i will discuss it.
islamophobia: i will reject it.
mental illness: i will not ignore it.

anti-Blackness: i will dismantle it.
abuse: i will call it out.
casteism: i will not stand for it.
sikhphobia: i stand by my kin.

i found my voice and i will use it.

Disconnection is lifelessness.
Silence breeds purposelessness in me.
I was not born, I do not live, I was not raised for silence.

chup kar.

this is the deep desi cultural conditioning that is locked in me.
it blocks me.

still, i will not look the other way.

log kya kahenge? i could care less what people think or say.
i refuse to align with the silencing chupkar ways of my people.

these toxic cultures of shame and silencing breed abuse.

i aim to be a cycle breaker.

elusive authenticity

a friend once remarked after tasting my daal, infused with
cumin and turmeric and stewed in tomato broth, that it was not
authentic. she offered me a recipe and her corrections. i declined.
people of multiple orientations and destinations are rarely "authentic."

we defy the sort of singularity that authenticity demands.

we are expected to fold the edges of ourselves into a single self.

we can not.

this is not our shortcoming.

when we learn to amplify the ingenuity of improvisation and
reinvention,
we overcome.

we reinvent the traditional daal and make it our own.

refusal is unbelonging

when we refuse or resist, we are no longer welcome. we
assimilate and twist ourselves into knots for the sake of
acceptance. after i spent much of my childhood obeying and
swallowing the fire of inquiry or rebellion, in my teen years, i
spoke up.

i was punished. i began to understand that refusal will have
consequences,
often dire.

refusal leads to disowning. to unbelonging.
who do you think you are? what's your aukat?

to be desi-ish
is to realize
that wherever desis reside,
caste-ism prevails.

Richard
Frankland

a meditation on lateral violence

lateral violence happens when we desi folks
identity police each other.
when we turn on each other
to protect whiteness.
when we internalize
the misleading narratives about us.
when one of us
is made to feel like they are not one of us.

when desi-ness
is weaponized by those who presume
to be the keepers of all that is desi.

there is no such thing. you are a fraud.

lateral violence happens so often in desi circles and
communities that i have come to expect it as the norm. diasporic
folks like me who have no other word or term to identify
ourselves, with roots in south asia but no fixed ties to the
subcontinent, are the targets of considerable lateral violence.
identity wounds are inflicted.

we are misnamed by our own communities. we are disowned in words and deeds. we are cut off from our roots by those who claim to have ownership of them. we are often told by our very own relatives that we have no right to the desh. we are reprimanded for being inauthentic. if we ever speak honestly about our heritage or utter words of caution about toxic cultural traits, we are shamed.

those of us who are also mixed or blended in our caste and faith identifications such as i am are often subject to identity exile. it is not unusual for well-educated and aware folks to misidentify my caste or misuse my identifications. they presume i am hindu. i am not. they do not consider how my baha'i faith interacts in complex ways with my family's caste of origin. identifications are fluid and nuanced within the vastness of what being desi means. most of us do not remember all this as we constrain and confine each other by performing lateral violence in the form of identity policing.

any wonder as a younger person, i distanced myself from my desi roots. this distancing is a form of self-harm. as i age, i have come to claim self-naming as a reclamation of my cultural heritage. how do fractured identities like mine evolve and grow?

bakwaas or pyar | बकवास or प्यार

to call out the bakwaas
in our cultural or discursive norms
results in being shunned and disowned.
we know that the moment

we utter even a mutter
of complaint or critique
of the ways in which
desi patriarchy colorism
aukaat oppressions
are abusive and harmful

we risk our belonging.
we must make brave choices:

chup kar and stay safely belonging
or speak out and risk unbelonging.

i made my choices.
no bakwaas
only radical revolutionary pyar
for self, sach, and haqq. सच | حقّ

mantra for speaking up

forget obedience.
forget politeness.
unlearn silence.
cultivate confidence.
speak from the heart.
raise your voice if you have to.
blow your own mind.

AFRICAN·ish

Indo-Africans

For hundreds of years, brown folks from the South Asian subcontinent have lived, thrived, and sometimes been exiled from Africa.

These peoples were referred to as Indo-Africans but not Afro-Indians.

Thanks to colonialism, "Indians" of various castes and faiths were forcibly brought to parts of Africa and the Caribbean from the 1860s onwards.

This complex history deserves its own chapter.

Indians Raced by Apartheid

During apartheid times in South Africa, a racial hierarchy was enforced:

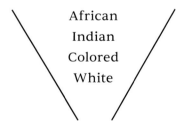

African
Indian
Colored
White

What is apartheid?

Apartheid happens where settler colonialism meets segregation meets enslavement.

All three oppressive systems intersected simultaneously to oppress the original keepers of the lands of southern Africa.

I was alive to witness both the deep systemic oppressions of apartheid and the revolutionary resistance movements across the border from Gaborone, only a few kilometers away from South Africa. Many of my classmates, neighbors, and teachers were South Africans of all hues and views about the apartheid regime. The South African Defense force would often raid our town in the middle of the night in search of folks who were suspected of being affiliated with the African National Congress. This terror resurfaces in my nightmares to this day.

Am I Motswana?

Botswana, in contrast to its neighbors in every direction, professed promises of racial harmony and tolerance.

It was said: We are not Rhodesia. We are not Namibia. We are not South Africa.

Kagiso. Peace lives here. We are democratic. All races live harmoniously here.

Truth is that we lived in the shadow of apartheid during the postcolonial land reform movements that took place as Rhodesia became Zimbabwe.

Truth is that we felt the reverberations of rebellion even in our kagiso-filled nation.

We witnessed the ravages of settler colonialism as we sheltered those in the resistance movements.

Tswana: land
Motswana: person from this land
Batswana: the people of this land
Setswana: the language of the people of this land

To be Motswana is not merely a statement of origin.

I am a person who comes from and was offered refuge in the sacred lands of the Tswana people. My family is not indigenous to Botswana. We are immigrants here. When my family was invited both to become honorary members of the Balete people by chosen family and offered citizenship here, this meant something so significant that I have never traded my Botswana passport for any other.

However, the question remains: Can people of Indian descent claim to be Batswana?

Frantz Fanon *For a colonized people the most essential value, because the most concrete, is first and foremost the land: the land which will bring them bread, and above all, dignity.*

Why am I African-ish?

For an Indian-descended citizen of Botswana like me to claim to be African-ish is equal parts

> + resistance to apartheid racial categories
> + commentary on the somewhat ridiculous nature of identity talk
> + dreaming of pan-African racial solidarity.

Maybe I am African-ish because I was born planted in East African soil, and grew shoots under the southern African sun. Although I was a brown seedling planted and replanted there, I am also an uprooted desi African.

I wish I were a rooted tree.
I wish to be a majestic baobab overlooking the glorious Zambezi.

In reality, I might be a healing tulsi herb in a clay pot perched precariously on a windowsill. My holy leaves would nourish and soothe ailments. I am certainly not the money plant desis cultivate in our homes for good luck.

Dominant narratives and counter narratives

All over Africa, there are sayings that translate as:
The story of the hunt is told by the hunter. Until the story of the hunt is told by the lion, we miss the full story.

(Hunter) What are the dominant narratives about African cultures, peoples, and places?
(Lion) What are some counter-narratives?

Debunking African stereotypes

All over the world, misinformation about Africa persists to this day. Wherever I travel, I am forced to defend or shed light on what growing up there is really like. These conversations are steeped in racist myths and single stories about Africa. There are so many widespread lies about Africa (the land, cultures, and peoples) that people hold as common knowledge.

Why must we debunk African stereotypes? Most of us have internalized them.

Frantz Fanon   *Imperialism leaves behind germs of rot which we must clinically detect and remove from our land but also from our minds as well.*

Africa is not a country

Word to the wise
from a person
born and raised
on the continent.

Africa is not a country.
Do not assume its uniformity.
Open your eyes
to its multitudes.

Africa is not a country.
Its multiple realities defy singularity.

Where?

Where are you from?

Gaborone.

Where?

(Breath.)

Botswana.

Where is that?

(Deep breath.)
Neighboring South Africa.
Oh. I thought it was next to Russia.

(Screams internally. Breath.)

It's in Africa.

Africa is not a country.

Exhausted confession:

Often, questions about where we are from are so exhausting, we skip the specificity and keep it general. As I scream internally, I can almost always predict that the person asking does not know where Gaborone or Dar es Salaam are. And once they learn, they can't imagine someone who looks like me would be from there.

Does everyone carry the burden of explanation like this?

Lost Daughter

I am a lost Daughter of Africa.
My soul home, Mother Africa, is calling me today.
It is Africa Day.
In my heart, every day is Africa Day.

Mother Africa beckons me daily.
She birthed me and raised me.
She schooled me and disciplined me.
She taught me that I am a brown daughter of the continent of
light.
She reminds me of my African names and tongues.

She beckons, "Nkai, wena tla kwano."
She whispers to my heart, "Almasi, kuja nyumbani...imekuwa
muda mrefu mno."

My heart responds by overflowing through my eyes.

I feel like a lost child of Mother Africa exiled to america.
Did I not choose this exile?

So many of us came here seeking
freedom
pursuing education
buying into capitalist models of success.

We lost our way as we
internalized that Africa doesn't matter.

We lost our way when we started to see Africa as a dark continent and deprived ourselves of her radiant light.

We lost our way every time our accents were mocked.

We lost our way every time our humanity was micro-aggressed.

We lost our remembrance of soulful joy as we were assailed by the single story of African danger, poverty, and backwardness.

We lost ourselves as we forgot to celebrate or ululate.

We got so very lost as we inhabited those neocolonizer beliefs.

We said it was survival.

We thought it was adaptation.

We weren't even conscious of losing ourselves.

We separate ourselves from that story of Africa.

We become aliens to Africa while being Aliens in america.

We suffer, often silently, the angst of Africa separation.

This is not your standard home sickness.
It is a soul wound, an illness.

My soul angst seeks for shadow comforts in bottomless cups of kahawa.

Memories of the endless flow of chai served to every guest.

I miss my folks who still reside on African soil.
I miss my Pa who is now one with Mother Africa, intermingled
with her earth as he wished.

I miss hearing the soul song sounds of greetings everywhere.
I miss the comfort of "Dumela, mma."

Ujambo? Habari?

O tsogile jang?

Ke la pile thata, bagaetso.
Nime choka sana hapa america.

I am soul tired here in america.
I yearn for the humanity that is Africa.
I'll put away the kahawa now and reach for the rooibos.

Cheers to Mother Africa on any given day
from a lost daughter yearning for home.

Playing and praying for belonging

The five-year-old me was straight up confused.

I was a brown African speaking Hindi to my parents who spoke
Punjabi to each other in private while we all spoke Kiswahili and
English in public.

We prayed interchangeably in English, Hindi, and Farsi.
We learned interchangeably in Kiswahili, Hindi, and English.
We played interchangeably in Kiswahili, Hindi, and English.
We ate ugali and daal and bhajiya and mandazi and most of all,
we relished ananasi sweeter than the sweetest pineapple you
ever did taste.

Saturday mornings at the beach nearby where Indian Ocean
breezes would lull us softly into relaxed exhales.
Madafu fresh coconut water sipped, we danced and swam in
sunny glee.

These flashes of childhood joys, of splashing
in carefree abandon, rolling around in beach sand remain with
me always.

The eight-year-old me was straight up flexible.
Come Sundays, we began our days chanting in Farsi and Arabic
at children's classes and devotions at the Bahá'í Center.

Next, we went, heads and legs covered, hearts reverent, to serve
and partake of the langar at the Gurudwara where our chacha
spent his days and some nights at the Khalsa club.
Where were our silver wrist adornments proving that we
belonged here?
I might have wondered in confused flexible silence.

I might have prayed for a kara of my own. ਕੜਾ

The ten-year-old me was straight up distressed at the temple as I

overheard adult murmurings in Gujarati about all of us fleeing to the West.
Hushed whispers in many languages, repeating that "Africa is for Black Africans."

It was time to leave this home. Where would we go?

The eleven-year-old me was disoriented as we bid farewell to days of Asante Sana, Ujambo, Habari? No more ananasi. No more Indian Ocean breezes.

The melodic words of childhood songs and prayers were soon left behind with confounded farewells.

Kwaheri.

The aunties and uncles murmured,

"We are no longer welcome here."

Did I pray I were Black so we might stay?
I just might have.

Kwaheri Tanzania, land of my birth, where I was told I did not belong.

Could we pray to stay?
Could we pray our way into belonging?

Soul-wounded, we left behind the days of playing and praying interchangeably in Hindi, Kiswahili, and English.
Quietly, in silence, we forgot the song-like sounds of karibu,

karibu.
Habari?

Kwaheri, land of my birth, that beckons me back whispering
soul yearnings for soul healings in my middle age.

We did not leave Africa. We headed south.
Southbound until we bypassed Rhodesia's colonialism and
knocked at apartheid's door.

Hodi. Hodi. (Do we hear a karibu?)

"Koko. Koko. Tsena," said Botswana.

The twelve-year-old me reluctantly learned to say "dumela."
The fourteen-year-old me straight up learned to call Mungu
Modimo.

I played hardly.
I prayed still.

Hai Raba, Allah, Mungu, god, Guru, Modimo,

I beseech all these years and all my days, Divine where I might
be.
The middle-aged me remembers how I played and prayed
through childhood
chaos, confusion, and quiet fear of un-belonging.
As I bear witness to the unfolding of colonizer terrorism
unleashed anew
on all of us others.
I know the terrors of unbelonging well.

They were my childhood companions.
Old soul wounds reopened today as I reside on american soil.

Belonging is unbelonging in belonging.

I ask Divine in all these tongues where I might belong.
Where is home for those of us never permitted to call any place
home?

She whispers to my ever broken heart, salve to my soul wounds:

"Child, you belong nowhere and so
you can abide anywhere and make a home everywhere."

So it is. So I be.

Longing for belonging

I pined for our previous home.
I longed to return.
My longing to belong
became an omnipresent heart song.

Persecution of faith minorities

I was raised among Iranian refugees. They fled faith-based persecution. They lost their loved ones, property, rights and resigned themselves to never going home. Among them, I learned to hide being Bahá'í. We did not mention it unless we were explicitly asked. When I do now, floodgates of inquiry or misunderstanding open wide.

Consent to enter

As an adult, I learned that many Indigenous peoples all over the globe seek consent before they enter lands where they do not reside. This is not just an ancient practice.

This is a practice I wish many immigrant settlers and travelers would adopt.

Forget a visa or work permit, what might immigration feel like if we actually asked consent to enter from the true keepers of the lands we visit or inhabit?

Consent to enter is what the call and response "Hodi. Karibu!" signifies.

Reconciling Harm

There are many stories to be told about how many nations, after formal colonial governance ended, resisted the presence of those brought to their lands by the colonizers.

People of Indian descent were brought to Africa for a specific colonial purpose.
We were master's tools.

If there were truth and reconciliation commissions for us, too, we would need to confess and be accountable for all the ways we brown folks perpetuate harms against the rightful keepers of the lands to which we were brought by colonial powers. This means that we became accustomed to using disciplinary and divisive tactics of the colonial authorities on each other.

We, brown folks, were master's tools.
We were employed to exert power over our Black compatriots.
Whether by force or by stealth, we abuse our Black kin.

Indo-Africans perpetuate harm on African lands.
Have we told this truth and reconciled?

Dis/ability

An invisible truth few people know about me is that I am an able-bodied first-born female child to two people with disabilities. In days when the term was not in question, they referred to themselves as handicapped.

I was raised to be a caregiver.

Western therapists told me I grapple with "survivor's guilt" as an adult because I have parents whose lives are informed and constrained by disability.

I struggled with shame because our family was so very differently abled.
In my youth, I resented having limitations and constraints that many of my peers did not. I pretended that disability did not matter.

When I grew up to develop (sometimes invisible) disabilities, I refused to accept them.

As an adult who studies western psychology, I learned our extended family suffered from intergenerational trauma, addiction, and mental illness.

It was denied in hushed tones, desi shame.
Disability within our family is profoundly complex.
I am constantly working to tell these stories about myself honestly even if I risk shame.

Here is one:

My Pa referred to himself as handicapped or disabled. He always claimed this identity unapologetically. For much of his life, he was an officer for the Botswana Society of People with Disabilities (BOSPED). All over Botswana, people recognize him as an engaged disabled citizen to this day. We would go places where he would inform folks who didn't yield to his needs that he was "digole," the Setswana word for disabled. To the embarrassment of his children, he would drive up to a parking lot and insist on parking near the entrance even if there were no designated parking spots for him. The parking attendants all over town would recognize his vehicle and wave him to his spot. He was blunt, direct, and shunned euphemisms when people mistreated him on account of his disability. I would cringe at these words and actions, and maybe despite knowing better, I still do.

He asked for help and sometimes demanded it from close folks and strangers alike. He used to say,

"I'm disabled. I have to ask for help. How else will I survive?"

How many of us see the light in this truth? I am still learning. I am still recovering and healing.

I often look back and wonder how I perpetuate ableism. Even if I know better, do I do better?

Home-ish

Something about being "home"–the home where my aging mother now resides–that brings me grief:

Even at home I am a misfit.

A blessing about Gaborone life is that I can leave for decades, but when I return, I am still oriented. I know where what is. I understand how things flow here. I hear words and see their meanings. I can make the collective gestures that those not from here will barely notice. I can bump into people I knew as a youth randomly in familiar places. Years go by and we can still recognize each other. It is truly a blessing to have a place like this where we can be visitors and right at home. If I'm not thinking about it, it's as if I've always been here.

Dumela.

I suppose this is the fleeting sense that many call home.

When I am here, I am home-ish.

So it is.

Dumela.

Where they see me as one of them

I have been blessed
to travel widely.
When I landed in Port of Spain, Trinidad,
my soul soared.
The immigration agent
glanced at me before examining my passport,
and simply said the words that resounded
like soul song,

"Welcome home."

I wept tears of relief and joy
intermingled with awe.

How can this be?
They even pronounce my name
as I wish it said,
effortlessly
as if I really am known here.

I am jubilant to know
that there are places in this expansive world
that I might yet discover
where the inhabitants might see me as one of them.

Glimpses of such blending in
I have been blessed with in South Africa,
throughout the Caribbean,
Indian Ocean isles,
Seychelles and Mauritius.

Diaspora.
And in some rare spaces intentionally curated by folks of color in the united states of america.

---

about me: a few more specifics

My father became a Bahá'í in the 1960's. He believed that educating girls was vital. He believed in seva and service. He embodied the Bahá'í teaching that work is worship. He worked long and hard. At the end of each day, when he removed his metal brace from his leg, his calloused feet were bruised and worn. He complained rarely. He swallowed his rage. Until it spilled out of him with volcanic force. Both my parents were educators. For a short spell, when my father studied at Rutgers for his Master's degree, he considered migrating to the united states in 1974. He returned to Tanzania because he said he did not wish to raise his children there. He mumbled about racist inequalities and how the Bahá'í faith teaches us the kind of racial harmony he enjoyed in East Africa.

He loved living in Tanzania and would not have left if the political situation had not forced us away. We fled south when other WaHindi left for Canada and the U.K.

Having cast aside his own ancestral faith to follow Bahá'í teachings, he embraced this faith community as his chosen family. The Bahá'í s from all over the world, but especially the refugees from Iran, became our community. We celebrated holy days and fasted in ways that affiliated us in desi eyes with Islam. Instead of denying these affiliations, we embraced ourselves with a deep sense of respect for Islamic culture and practices.

Where we rest in peace

Pa's extended family could not comprehend why he would decline the Hindu last rites of his ancestors. He requested in his will that we lay him to rest in peace in Botswana. He specified that he was not to be cremated.
If he is buried there, isn't this the place I ought to consider my home?

Who taught me to embrace myself?
Who taught me to accept myself?

Who taught me to embrace humanity?

Me? Simply.
Ubuntu. Botho.

We were taught from an early age that motho ke motho ka batho.
A person is a person among people.

In my Pa's papers after his passing, I found old photographs. One
depicts me as an infant, cradled in the arms of a young woman
no older than nineteen or twenty.

Dada

I wonder...

I always knew in my heart that I was raised and loved and
lullabied and rocked and sung to by "dada."
      I see that I truly was.

I don't know your name but if my Pa were living, he'd tell me all
about you
and your people.
I knew you were a member of our family.
I imagine you wrapped me in a kanga cloth and tied me to your
back while you swept or washed or cleaned.
I know you bathed and dressed me.
The buttons and hooks weren't easy for my mama, paralyzed on
her right side, to manage on her own.
You were her extra pair of hands.

I imagine you took me on walks to admire the lands.
I feel deep in my soul the love planted in me for this land that
calls me back to it now and still.
I imagine you hummed melodies in Kiswahili that lulled me into
restful slumber.

Did you teach me to honor and respect Black Africans like yourself?
Did you tell me stories of your life in Shinyanga?
Did you remind me in warning tones that WaHindi like me
weren't always kind to your kind?

      I wasn't to be like that.

I know this lesson well, but I have always wondered where I first
learned it.
Your kind and knowing eyes tell me that you might have reared
me with life-long soul lessons.

Did you call me by my Kiswahili name?

Almasi. Diamond.
Did I have words to call you dada?
Asante sana, dada. Wherever you are.

This is Almasi cared for and raised by you in 1972.
How can I voice my thanks to you?

  Nime sahao jina lako lakini tena
  Nakumbuka yale uliyonifundisha.

Wherever you are, I remember what you taught me.

I love and honor my kin with all my heart and soul.
I know where I came from.
   I know who nurtured and raised me.
I dream that one day, I will find, meet and thank you.

Adopted kin

All over the lands where I grew up, people adopted, raised, and lived in kinship arrangements with folks not related to them. My friends lived with their aunts in the city in order to attend school there. My neighbors adopted their distant cousin because his family passed away from an illness we rarely named that ravaged southern Africa in the eighties and nineties. Many acquaintances orphaned by this epidemic were raised by extended community members.

People create kinship

Sometimes, those who resided in one family home were bound to each other in relations of servitude. While anti-Blackness often inhibited Indo-Africans from claiming kinship, the grace of folks who abided by ubuntu community care ethics adopted me and my family into their own.

Chosen family

Stories of the kinship bonds between people of different races all over the African continent are rarely told. While it is true that racial hierarchies exist and persist, it is also true that people are adopted into chosen family structures. My father's closest friend, Barnabas, was a refugee from Sudan residing in Dar es Salaam. He referred to my pa as "my brother." He bestowed our family with a special place in his family's rituals. Steadfastly, even now, my mother would tie or mail a rakhee for him. We were bonded. I would grow up to do the same for my adopted older brother, who I affectionately call Abuti. I send him a sacred thread each year.

In Botswana, one of my father's students invited him home to visit her family. Her elders declared that my father was "one of them." They walked to a corner of their family compound and gifted it along with two goats to my pa. Pa understood that this privilege came with responsibility. He honored it by visiting the elders, sending funds, and showing up to family gatherings and consultations. These elders gave us each names and mine is Nkai.

When I married, this aunty performed the Tswana wedding duties of a rakgadi for me. My own buas from Delhi did not attend.

about me

I was born on the cusp of Cancer and Leo. I am neither crab nor lion. I might be both.

Even the stars aligned on the night of my birth as if to predict that I would have unsteady destiny.

If I were to reincarnate, I would be a morni. I am a strange bird. Peafowl remind me of me.

I have tender and fleeting memories of childhood in Dar es Salaam.

I recall flashes of joyful running along the beach with parents who did not swim watching from afar. We sipped fresh madafu coconuts and inhaled the earthy aroma of roasting mihogo cassava.

Home life was turbulent. My parents were often at odds with one another.

School was a respite. I learned my lessons well.

The textbooks and school books were imported from India. The High Commission taught us patriotism, Sanskrit, and history of a land far away.

We knew India as a place to visit relatives we barely knew. We knew India through the aerogramme letters delivered each month, brimming with handwritten news from the relatives or rakhis or requests.

I was an accident-prone child. I was wounded often, not always by chance. My body bears more scars from stitches than I can count. I wear long pants and maxi dresses to hide the scars of my childhood.

Scars

It's time we talk about our scars and let the world see them.
I have many scars.
I have a gash above my right eyebrow, well-hidden by my hair
pulled over my forehead, just so.
Makeup dabbed and covered, just so.

Recess. Running. Chasing. Running.
Bam. Slam.
Sharp edge of the building.

The chasers stopped cold.
School uniform bleached white drenched redder than red.
I don't recall if I cried. I don't remember the pain.

I do remember my nervous mother was the only driver.
She, accompanied by the strict principal, drove me
trembling trembling shaking shaking, wavering but brave to the
Agha Khan Hospital.

Because love.

Dar es Salaam circa 1979.
Stitched up.
They said the gash was deep and needed double stitches.
They said I could've lost my right eye.
The doctor instructed my vegetarian mother to feed me chicken
soup because I was so weak and had lost so much blood.
This vegetarian mama went searching for chicken soup and
tried to feed it to me.

Because love.

I denied the chicken soup.
Because I'm like that and always have been.
I healed.
I could see again.
Scarred.
Cautious at recess, but I ran and chased and played again.

It's time we talk about our scars and let the world see them.
These scars hold stories of love and fear and healing and love.

Childhood trauma?

A therapist once informed me that I had PTSD due to
childhood trauma.
I chuckled in disbelief
wondering why I had to pay for this obvious diagnosis.
Then, I asked, what is the remedy?
Silence ensued.

Vote?

Election Day in Botswana.
I am 49 years old. I have never voted.
I was born in Tanzania, a country that did not validate my citizenship.
For much of my life, I carried the passport of my Indian heritage but not my belonging.
When I was a college student, my family became citizens of Botswana where we resided and which we considered our "forever home."
I was living as a student with an F-1 visa in america then.
I reside in the united states now. My status here is complicated at best. I came here as an F-1.
Then, I became an H-1B. Authorized to be employed. Legal.
After I married an american, it took me many years to get a "green card."
I have not seriously considered becoming a citizen.
I take pride in my Botswana passport. Becoming a voting american was neither my aim nor aspiration.
But on election day, I wish I could vote in my naturalized home country alongside my Batswana kin for democracy's sake.
I could never vote in Tanzania, the land of my birth.
I've never voted in India (or Pakistan for that matter), the land of my ancestry.
I've never been in Botswana during an election cycle. I wish I could be teleported to an election booth.

In america, I do not have the right to vote.
Maybe I never will?
Even though I shun flag-waving patriotism,

I wish I could vote.
Until we build another world and another system,
I trust that though the vote is not a revolution, it matters.

Maya Angelou   *Words are things. You must be careful, careful*
about calling people out of their names, using
racial pejoratives and sexual pejoratives and all that
ignorance. Don't do that. Someday, we'll be able to
measure the power of words.

A diamond in name

My Swahili name is Almasi.
I was born in a diamond mining town,
Shinyanga, Tanzania.
I moved to Gaborone, Botswana.
Diamonds are the single major source of our wealth.
Batswana take tremendous pride in our diamonds.
We chuckle when we tell the story
of how the British left our land
in 1966
only months before diamonds were discovered
in the depths of our soil.

When strangers
quiz me
about African droughts and poverty
I eye them quizzically

and warn them of
the dangers of a single story.

Africa is diamond rich.

Diamonds worth

Born and raised where diamonds are mined,

I adorn my body with amber, agate, and amethyst.

I know that muti magic is crystallized.

I was taught that I am mine-rich in gems of inestimable value.

No jewel's worth compares to honesty, truth, and integrity.

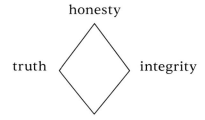

Expat

What does it mean to always be an expatriate and rarely be considered a patriot?

I grew up in Shinyanga, Dar es Salaam, and Gaborone. With the exception of a brief time as a toddler in Chandigarh in the maternal grandparents' home, I did not know India as a home.

We were expats. We had work permits with expiration dates. I recall how every two to three years, my parents' worry and uncertainty resurfaced. Would we need to return to Delhi? What would we even do there? None of us remembered how to live or earn a living there. We prayed, hoped, and did our earnest best to be good guests worthy of contract renewals. Pa worked long hours with exemplary dedication. My parents served with the kind of seva ethic that all their faith and cultural practices revered. Pa would say, "work is worship." Ma would reply, "seva is the only way."

What does being a brown expat mean? It is a precarious life, living caught in the balance, knowing that the advantages we might enjoy are temporary and incomparable to those of the European and american expats. We rarely speak of these inequities as we are supposed to be grateful immigrants.

As a child of Indian expats, I learned that we do not buy furniture. We do not invest resources in material objects that do not fit into suitcases. We do not have heirlooms. We are ready to pack everything we need into two suitcases, twenty kilos each.

We know that we are guests here. We are ever uncertain as we are wishful that we could call here, wherever here may be, home.

Wazungu

I was taught to defer to the wazungu.
We pleased the wazungu.
We were not to be cheeky to them.
The repercussions could be dire.
We swallowed our pride and dimmed our dignity.
We appeased the wazungu.

Somehow, we held on to our humanity.

What does caping for whiteness look like?

Africans Abroad?

We live in a world where a Botswana-based official media outlet promotes a blogger called "The Blonde Abroad."
Nobody blinks. They applaud that a westerner has deemed their land travel-worthy.

When a passport-carrying brown citizen asks why we seek such foreign validation, she is accused of being racist. She is mocked and questioned.
She is interrogated by white South Africans who live in Botswana.

I am she. I am the African abroad who is tired of inhabiting a world in which we of the African soil are oblivious to the histories and presence of colonialism and imperialism.

When I point out that brown and Black folks who live on the African continent center whiteness because of internalized oppression, I am negated.

I refuse to cape for whiteness in the motherland.
I am tired of the violence done daily to Black and brown bodies globally.

Why, pray tell, is an official Botswana outlet promoting the blog posts of a white person from California?

Why promote this white person's neocolonial fantasy of Africa?

When I inquire, I am called a racist.

Ngũgũ wa Thiong'o   *Let us call people by what they call themselves.*

A matter of names

Names matter.
In the cultures of places where I have lived,
names are infused with value
and fused with values.

Given names

My sibling, niblings, and children have been given
Tswana names.

Tumelo: Faith
Tirelo: Service
Kagiso: Peace
Akanya: To think

Internalized colonialism

Subjects like me are objects of colonial intervention. We often consume ideologies, practices, and belief systems that perpetuate harm against ourselves and others. Often, we learn how to be colonial subjects through western style schooling. Schooling colonizes our minds, bodies, and spirits.

The legacy of colonialism is alive.
Decolonization has many meanings.
It is not an event. To me, it is a holistic process.
It means redressing the damage to our cultures and ideas as much as to our lands and histories.

Ngũgũ wa Thiong'o   *The most important area of domination was the mental universe of the colonized, the control through culture of how people perceived themselves and their relationship to the world.*

Paolo Freire   *There's no such thing as neutral education. Education either functions as an instrument to bring about conformity or freedom.*

Re-Educated

Schooling would liberate us.
Education frees, I was told.
I learned my lessons well.
I was the A-student.
I believed that this would guarantee me
a freer, fuller life.
Until, upon reading Freire, I was stunned to discover
that the schooling I underwent was designed by
colonizers to keep me in my place.
I was to learn of daisies and daffodils
growing in prairies, meadows, and hills
that I might dream of,
but never enter.
I was to become one of the gatekeepers for my own.

Visa denied.
Madam, you may not enter the United Kingdom.
I had the Cambridge certificates, but was denied the diploma.
This is the ironic education of a post-colonial subject like me.
We are educated to be subjugated in a world that denies our
humanity.

So began an unlearning.
A re-education.
A reorientation.
I call this personal decolonization.

European Inquisitions

Let me tell you about the time that I made the error of speaking French to an immigration agent in Brussels.

This was 1990. I carried a valid passport. My plane ticket sent me from Johannesburg to Brussels. An overnight layover was planned in Brussels. I had proof of an onward ticket to the united states of america. I possessed a student visa (F-1). I had enough cash to pay for the hotel and snacks to boot. I had planned an evening of strolling through the European city I had read about, but never visited. I intended to sample some chocolate.

Earlier that year, I had spent six weeks of language immersion in France. I had then visited Haifa for a Bahá'í pilgrimage.

The immigration agent saw too many red flags to pass me through to entry.

He called over his supervisor, and in French that I understood, said that surely, I was a spy. I had an Indian passport and had just spoken to him clearly in French. The supervisor thought something of this theory, so as an eighteen-year-old, I was ushered to an inquisition room where I was questioned at length about my immigration status, and where I was really from. I decided to speak in crystal clear British English. I insisted I was an eager tourist. I was an america-bound student. I was eighteen.

They saw me as a spy. They did not see me as a global traveler. They did not see me as a curious youth. They were stumped by my passport and the stamps it held.
The inquisition, with no parent to call or stranger to assist me,

lasted several hours.

When I arrived at my hotel, I was too fatigued to explore. I admired the architectural beauty from afar as I suspected I would not enjoy this place up close. I smelled the stench of xenophobia lurking in European finery. Did I sample the chocolate? I do not recall. If I did, it was not memorable.

And, from this gruelling experience, I learned to never be too keen to speak French or reveal how much I understand to folks who hold privilege. I have now become the person who eavesdrops on conversations in multiple languages, French, Hindi, Punjabi, Kiswahili, Setswana, even Farsi and Spanish with a straight face, not revealing my comprehension.
I do not reveal how much I follow and how much I wish to join these conversations. I listen.

I rarely, if ever, let on how much I know and where I have been.

Thanks to the immigration officers in Brussels, I have also learned to disarm white inquisition with finesse worthy of a spy.

Postcolonialism is a lie

There is no post
to colonialism.
Don't believe me?

RESEARCH:
Missionization
Colonial education
Voluntourism

International Development
Industrial Complex
Aid Industrial Complex
White Savior Complex

My own saviorism

To be raised on African soil,
is to intimately know
that a form of global white supremacy
lurks everywhere in the continent.

International development agencies
church groups
global fundraisers
experts descend upon Africa and Asia,
seeking to save "underdeveloped nations"
from our own presumed backwardness,
while defiling our lands
with their misinformed prescriptions.

This is the way of the saviorism,
that is so often rooted in us insidiously.
Permanent damage under the guise of good intentions.

We, the saved, become saviors.
I strive to unlearn the forms of saviorism
I inadvertently adopted when I was schooled
in the West.

Who taught me to know myself?
Who taught me about myself?
Who taught me to learn myself?

Postcolonial Africa is a neocolonial Africa, too.

We were taught by whiteness culture and whiteness curricula and people of whiteness. Many of my teachers were white South Africans who both condemned apartheid and were shaped by it. Growing up in the shadow of apartheid and raised in desi communities, I came to know caste and racial hierarchies intimately. Even if I did not have the words to convey my lived experiences of racism and casteism in sociological terms, I understood what they looked and felt like.

Trauma memory

i am a hyphenated human. i am punctuated human. i am a human ever chasing my humanity...

there is enough childhood trauma and racial trauma and immigrant trauma and interpersonal trauma and relational violence trauma and healthcare discrimination trauma and we disown you trauma and fired trauma and unfairly treated trauma and gender based assault trauma and and and trauma for which there are only neurological symptoms and

memory lapses that i write myself into healing on these pages with

g a p i n g   g a p s

s i l e n c e s

l a p s e s

t h a t   c a n   a s   y e t   n o t   b e

r e m e m b e r e d

r e c a l l e d

o r   h e a l e d .

I am often asked why I write in these half sentences lacking form and essay-like clarity. I cannot tell you exactly the moment when my body was shocked by blows. I cannot detail to you how the realities of being told that Africa was only for Africans dawned on our family. I cannot recount too many stories of childhood revelry that are not shadowed by family trauma. My parents were refugees who lived with disabilities and they were unable often to put words to the traumas their bodies and minds held. They came undone. There is no clarity of memory in me to say why I can barely recall my days in Tanzania or India. Trauma memory is suppressed for survival.

I am asked why I write half thoughts seemingly inconclusive. I say trauma memory is like this. There is much I have yet to name or process or heal.

The forms of communication of translated, hyphenated, and punctuated humans are slippery, flowing, contradictory, evasive, messy.

Tripod pots

When people speak of their immigrant journeys, we often say we are caught between two worlds and two languages and two cultures.

I am like the tripod pot set outside with a fire lit under it.

These are the heavy cast iron pots with three legs holding them steady even as we fill them with metsi and motogo to stir with wooden spoons to make our morning porridge. We gather the firewood from nearby and tend the flame under the steady but hot pot.

I feel like I am a tripod hot pot.

Silence as a love language

There are some intimate truths about my life that cannot as yet be spoken even by someone outspoken. These truths will be tucked away because even as I urge myself and others to speak up and speak out, I am keenly aware of the contradictory insight I offer:

Silence can be a radical love language, too.

To be African-ish
is to know that my father, the first immigrant to Africa in his family, as I am the first to be born there, wished to be buried in this home.

To be African-ish
is to know intimately the multiple
tones and faces and voices
of xenophobia.

To be African-ish
is to be a brown minority
in a land colonized by white Europeans
who left a legacy of racial hierarchy
in which I am precariously placed.

To be African-ish is to be intimately acquainted with colonialism and imperialism.

It is to be educated in the language of the masters
and graded by the standards of the colonizers.

To be African-ish
is to often hear from Europeans and Australians
that racism is unique to america.

To be African-ish
is to be presumed uncivilized,
ironically, even by skinfolks who
were taught the single false story
that Africa is just a land of deprivation and poverty.

To be a human raised on the African continent
is to know that where colonial oppressions prevail
we fight tooth and nail.

Resistance and revolutions also prevail.

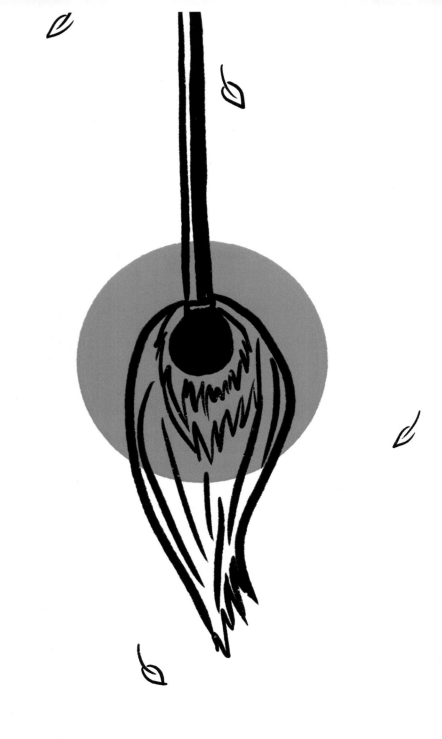

AMERICAN·ish

Wonder

I often wonder, "what is the matter with me that I do not belong?"
Even in a land considered a melting pot, place of dreams, I am a misfit.

These doubts were born of the taunts that plagued my youth.
These were the unsung struggle songs of my heart and soul.

I wonder and I wander.

i. REVELATIONS

The oppressive political system of the united states of america is described by bell hooks as:

Imperialist white-supremacist capitalist patriarchy.

Audre Lorde teaches:
There is no such thing as a single-issue struggle because we do not live single-issue lives.

Toni Cade Bambara testifies:
I've never been convinced that experience is linear, circular, or even random. It just is. I try to put it in some kind of order to extract meaning from it, to bring meaning to it.

I often exclaim:

america is a helluva ride.
Every time a new injustice unfolds, I say:
america is on brand.
american-brand capitalism sucks
my life force.
Every now & again, I awake to dismay:
america is a dumpster fire.

     The pages that follow are my ride on these lands.
I've been knotted up, exhausted, oppressed & traumatized
while learning, hopeful, protesting & audacious.
There are struggle songs & protest verses.
There are lessons & blessings.

Chimamanda Ngozi Adichie *There is no single story here.*

To be an american-ish immigrant
is to live & breathe daily with
weighty questions & reminders that
belonging is unbelonging in belonging.
To be here
is to reside on the land whose keepers
are the Muscogee (Creek).
but as an immigrant,
I was almost forty years old
when I first heard this land acknowledgement.
To be here
is to be educated
& to hold multiple degrees
from elite institutions that pride themselves
on their global acclaim.
To be here
is to know that I hold
considerable educational privilege
while being minoritized
& presumed inadequate
despite my verifiable advanced global competence.
To be here
is also to be keenly aware
that brown people
end up in cages & on the other side of walls.

Words like weapons for others

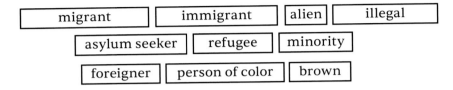

They use these words like weapons
to divide, remove & cage us.

american geography

I land in Houston after taking a group of undergraduate students
to Trinidad for a cultural immersion trip. I do not fly with a
U.S. passport. Though I have recently experienced the ease of
arriving in Port of Spain & blending in, I am still prepared for a
different kind of welcome in Houston. Head covered, I approach
the immigration officer with a bright smile & greeting. Batswana
taught me well that greeting is a way of seeing humanity & there
are no strangers in life if we greet each other with a nod or part
with blessing. I imagine singing, "Dumela, rra." But instead I
offer up my passport with a simple smile.

The invented categories in immigration forms have real
consequences.
The officer pauses. It is a long pause.

He glances at me. He glances at the passport.
"Earth calling Houston," I say in jest in my head.

Oh, yes, I am oriented. I have arrived in Houston & I cannot wait to return to Atlanta to hug my children again after a long week of constant teaching.

After what seems like an extended examination of my documents–green card scanned, my photo taken–I am asked to present my hands for fingerprinting.

I comply.

I do not have passport privilege. I am accustomed to such inquisitions in airports.
Trinidad truly was a relief. No extra red tape. No visa needed. No proof of funding.

Welcome home?
I will not receive this greeting here. I know this.

The agent raises his eyebrows after all the formality and inquires, "Where is Botswana?"

I am a teacher. I am an educator. My knee-jerk response is to throw a question back at him. He is a federal employee charged with weighty decisions about who enters U.S. borders. Shouldn't he know basic world geography?

This is america. He has no clue. Before I can swallow my humor, I invite him to guess.

He stares back with no humor & no conjecture.

The pause is long until I inform him that I could not help my teacher instincts & yes, I am a brown African because Botswana is a southern African nation.

He does not blink. He does not smile. He simply hands me back my passport & green card (to my relief) & states, "I have never seen one of these before."

I exhale. I sigh. I do not allow him to see me cringe.
americans, do your homework.

I'm feeling quite like an alien again. Still.
So many inquisitions & interrogations leave me depleted.
So many looks & stares find me exhausted.

What are you?

How come you are African but you say you are not African-american?
What is apartheid?
Would you consider running for public office?
I assumed you were american. Don't you act like an american?
Where are you really from?
What's a critical language?
Why do you even live in the U.S.?
What's an F-1?
Don't you have a green card? You're set then, right?
Why didn't you just get naturalized to be an american?
Why don't you celebrate Christmas?
How does the travel ban even affect you?

What does being a Baháʼí have to do with the countries on the travel ban list?
So does that mean you're actually Muslim?
Why do you sometimes cover your head?
What is wrong with being a migrant? Aren't you a migrant?
What does "mother of Black children" even mean?
If you're not american & you can't vote, why can't you contact your senators anyway?

An inquiry is not an inquisition.

If they think they know me, chances are they've been assuming quite a bit & hardly know me at all.

When asked sincerely, I'm happy to answer these questions & tell them some stories, too.

The relentless questions are an inquisition.
My answers to these questions:

I'm the kind of "other" who could very easily & for many different reasons end up on a list or on the other side of a wall.

I am not alone.

There are many "others" just like me.

We got us.

Who taught me to translate myself?
Who taught me to assimilate myself?
Who taught me that adjacency is belonging?

My coming to america

Many of us who enter the united states learn the code words & legalities of immigration quickly. F-1. H-1B. Green card. Naturalized citizen.

Immigrants often pay attention to the nuances & differences in the types of immigration journeys, choices & realities among us. Those who call us immigrants assume a uniformity of experience that is often elusive.

What we often fail to come to terms with is how we folks from the majority world, from the two thirds world, often misnamed Third World, are consumed & co-opted by the american empire. Some political theorists have named this phenomenon the periphery within the center.

People like me are the margins & peripheries existing within the centers of empire.

Much of my life on american soil is deeply informed by learning the intimacies of white supremacy even as I become entangled with it.

Many of the folks who immigrated here become white adjacent. I could be. I have been at times.

From the moment I landed in the united states, I recognized familiar forms of colonization and apartheid here.

I recognize a settler colonial state fronting as a self-professed democracy.

The pressures to become white adjacent remain omnipresent.

I continue to resist. When we arrive, model minority myths are sold & fed to us. These stories constrain us. They indoctrinate us into assimilation while othering us into oppression.

We are required to translate & transmute ourselves even as we must build ourselves into bridges for others to cross over to see, recognize & know us.

Many folks of color refer to university campuses as modern day plantations. In the mouths of whiteness, sending us back to the plantation is a weaponized reality.

———

F-1

International Student
Non-immigrant
deemed worthy of entering
the US of A
to study.
But first you need to pass the
TOEFL.
Test of English as a Foreign Language.
You may not enter
on an F-1 visa
unless you pass this test.
Do U.S. students take this test?

Of course not.
They speak English.
Plus, you have extra hurdles.
But first you need to prove
that you have enough cash in the bank
to pay your way
because it is more than likely
you are not eligible for funding.
You will pay to subsidize
the education of those
who speak English.
F-1
You don't know this yet:
Kehinde Andrews the University
is still a plantation.
You will learn this quickly.
No bootstrap myth,
no assimilative tricks,
no faith in the american dream
will prepare you
for the
F-1 Life
of indentured servitude
on the University plantation.
You might even deny it
& suffer in silence
because you were told
when you applied
& were granted
the sought after
F-1
to be grateful

to be very grateful
for the opportunity.
To pay tuition
while being exploited
silenced
denied
& oppressed
by systemic xenophobia
& isms countless
that make you feel less than.
You will even be subjected
to English only
rules of comportment.
Be glad & grateful
you are an
F-1
on this plantation.
You will learn that
your dismal fate is
considerably or marginally
better off than
Black
Indigenous
Muslim
& Undocumented
folks.
You might even slip
& fall
into the plantation life
by becoming complicit in the
oppressions of
those marginally worse off than you.

You might be tricked
into believing that this proximity
will earn you a free pass
but alas, you've been fooled.
F-1, non-immigrant
student
be grateful
speak English
or go back to where you came from.

June, 2017:

To be me is to accumulate enough educational privilege
to learn enough antiracism
that my speaking out calling out
renders me unemployable
even in academia
where free speech is supposedly upheld.

———

Spaces & places where I have labored

University of Chicago
Stanford University
Spelman College
Agnes Scott College

For almost two decades of my life, I considered college campuses home-like. I was lulled by their quirky charms & architecture. I was lured in by their fancy gardens & manicured landscapes. I was attracted to the energy of youth & curiosity. I was sucked into the majestic libraries. I was embraced by the silent promises of knowledge. I enjoyed wielding the ID cards & keys to basement libraries. I relished hauling stacks of books & notebooks from one classroom to the next. I imagined that nobody would question my presence there. I earned access to Greek lettered societies with secret handshakes. I would fade into the scenery. I was consoled by predictable practices. I was willing to overlook the slights & dismissals. I had faith in my own studiousness. I later realized that I had so much of my worth & identity tied up in scholarship & being an educator. These identities stifled me.

I am no longer drawn to college campuses. I no longer belong there.

Human dictionary

No dictionary definitions are required.
I know these words as experiential vocabulary

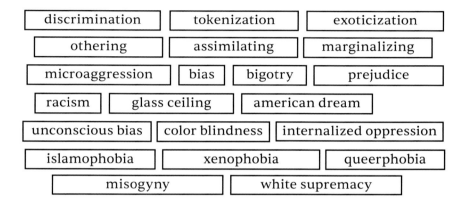

discrimination	tokenization	exoticization
othering	assimilating	marginalizing
microaggression	bias	bigotry	prejudice
racism	glass ceiling	american dream
unconscious bias	color blindness	internalized oppression
islamophobia	xenophobia	queerphobia
misogyny	white supremacy

Some may require a dictionary.
I am a living breathing surviving
illustrated exemplified
dictionary of -isms personified.

I am also a human diary
whose pages are overflowing
with courage, resilience,
means to cope,
will to hope
& resistance
to -isms.

Immigrant explanations

I am weary.
Immigration is often a privilege.
Those who only see a brown body do not care how I came
to be here.
It is also true: to those unfamiliar, who care less for
distinction,
is there a difference between
a South Asian &
a Central American?
If I were driving down the street &
ICE pulled me over,
would it matter what kind of brown
I am?
Maybe.
Maybe not.

Immigrant invisibility

americans who aren't americans
We the immigrants
We live here
We work here
We might even bear children who are from here
But we are always the "other"
Ever ever the other
We don't get to belong here
We are erased from belonging
& we do not have any other place to call home
americans who aren't americans

We are here
We live here
We work here
We might even bear children who try to belong here
So, we are neither here nor there
We are other
We are ether
We are vapor

Here.
Not here.
You see? We are invisible
americans who aren't americans
We the immigrants are invisible
& even so, you seek to erase us.

Betita Martínez   *South Asians end up in cages, too, you know.*
Oppression Olympics are not going to free us, though.
How do we solve xenophobia & seek justice in
immigration for us all?

———

Am I a global citizen?

I no longer describe myself this way even though others might.
I learned that these universal concepts are often steeped in
neoliberal ideals that are white-centering. Who is the default
global citizen? Who is excluded?
Talk of world unity & human oneness can often erase
marginalized folks. Such calls for unity without addressing
systemic inequities are harmful.
Who does global citizenship benefit? Who is erased?

Who taught me to erase myself?
How did I learn to hide myself?
Who taught me to be my full self?

My american dream

In the united states of america, immigrants who enter with
no nuanced knowledge of the history of this nation's settler
colonialism & white supremacy are bound to become new
settlers. We erase the histories of Indigenous & Black folks as we
settle here on lies sold as american dreams of better living.
I came with dreams of higher education & plans to return to the
lands of the Tswana or Sotho or Zulu. I did not dream to stay. I
dreamed of a life of seva & tirelo to the peoples who invited us
expats to become naturalized citizens. I dreamed of learning
skills that I would pack into my brain. I would pack my life into
two suitcases (twenty kilos each) to carry homeward. Was I
cautioned that I would get trapped here? I do not recall. Perhaps,
I did not heed the warnings. My american dream was to leave
america as soon as I possibly could. Every now & then, I dream
this dream.

about me: a few recent specifics

I came to the united states to pursue higher education.
I was an academic scholarship student.

My parents, salaried civil servants & educators, could not afford to pay for higher education abroad. I worked as a child caregiver & tutor to support myself.

I intended to return to my parents after college as they expected.
I met my beloved & reason to remain here. I conceived my children & birthed them here.

I have resided in the Atlanta area longer than anywhere else. My children were both born in the city of Atlanta, not far from where their father grew up. Their grandparents' home is a place of regular visits & steadiness for us. My in-laws were educated at historically Black colleges. They have roots & legacy here in Atlanta, GA.

There are so many versions of me. I stay here in part because I like the freer version of myself I am becoming here.

I reside in america because my children & their kin are here.
Is their home also my home?

an american realization:
I am in an abusive relationship with america.

———

Dehumanizing of Othering...

Us	them
Us	Citizens
Us	Immigrants
Us	Illegals
Us	Undocumented
Us	Non-citizens
belong	un-belong
here	there
human	un-human?

Othering makes us versus them.
Othering builds

Walls
Borders
Separations.
Othering
Confines
Violates
Kills.
Othering
Dehumanizes while justifying
a falsely constructed Us.

There are no others when we are all Human.

July, 2017:

The everyday suffering of brown & Black folks often does not make the nightly news.

———

On being an Aunty Professor

I contracted many ailments while other
in academia.
PTSD.
Migraines.
Severe Vertigo.
Autoimmune disorders.
Imposter Syndrome.
Panic attacks.
Insomnia.

All these ailments paled in comparison
to the abuse in the form of
the push & pull
that resulted in
a simultaneous parading of my body
while I was subtly
silenced
undermined
discounted
told I was not enough.

I died an academic death
from a thousand cuts
that led to a lay-off.

With all the outward diversity touting
posturing
that claimed that those embodied
as other
as me
were welcome on campus,
the ailment that I contracted
while employed as an alternative track academic
was the deep seated academic precarity
that comes from outward valuation
while being covertly erased.

Laid off.
I was erased.
I was removed.
I was expelled.
I was exiled.
The higher ups claimed, "this lay-off is not a
reflection of your work."
I knew my worth &
I knew the work
invisible to most
that went into sustaining my wholeness.

I left
with a severe case of academic PTSD
and a case of academic precarity
in which diversity is valued
but I am erased.

If it were not for the hundreds of
former students

who bemoaned aloud my academic death
& still call me Aunty or Professor
I'd be completely undone.
So I live on to heal
in exile
away from academia
to reconcile myself
with my worth and work.

August, 2017:

Sometimes we are blamed & shamed for systemic injustice or discrimination. What is a personal failure & what is not my doing?

———

Unbelonging is my vibe

Those of us fluent in the language of belonging,
comprehend that silence, pauses, tone, inflection
are just as potent in signaling
      belonging or unbelonging
as words themselves.

UNBELONGING

DISCUSS:

Pyramid of
White Supremacy

Overt white supremacy

Covert white supremacy

White supremacy culture

ii. CONVERSATIONS

W.E.B. Du Bois *What do we want?...We want to be americans, full-fledged americans, with all the rights of other american citizens. But is that all? Do we want simply to be americans? Once in a while through all of us there flashes some clairvoyance, some clear idea, of what america really is. We who are dark can see america in a way that white americans cannot. And seeing our country thus, are we satisfied with its present goals and ideals?*

James Baldwin *I love america more than any other country in the world, and exactly for this reason, I insist on the right to criticize her perpetually.*

Roxane Dunbar-Ortiz *Not a nation of immigrants.*

Who is Blindian?

This is a relatively new term used to describe my family. In our family, one parent is Black and another is from the Indian subcontinent. My children of both desi and Black heritage may be called Blindian.

December, 2017:

I have lost count of the times I have been asked to show people how to have conversations about race and racism.

———

Parenting Black children while brown

When my daughter was three, a child she was playing with informed her that she did not play with brown-skinned girls. When my child informed me of this, I went to her teacher who informed me that my child was mistaken. It happened again & then again. At the same school, a few years later, my son was called the n-word by his classmates. When he reported it to the teacher, she accused him of fabricating the situation for attention. When it happened again & I intervened, these teachers defended the other children & accused my child of multiple transgressions. In this ongoing parenting journey, on the job, I learned that anti-Blackness begins early. By the time they were in first grade, both my children had faced the n-word directed at them. The deep seated denial by educators & white parents of these realities are oppressive.

I paid tuition to an elite school that valued time in nature, hikes & woodwork but conversations around race were deemed divisive. Those targeted by racism had no recourse. Every attempt to redress these harms was met with denial or worse. I resorted to amplifying conversations in our home, in earnest, about race & identity. I could not prepare or shield my children for what we might encounter in classrooms, baseball fields, gardens, & even friends' homes, but I could be sure that they understood who they are & how not to internalize the -ism projected onto them because of their skin color. In our home, we talk often & openly about racism. We take pride in our blended identities. We advocate for our Black kin. We defend our humanity by refusing to enter spaces where our spirits are harmed.

We do not sugarcoat the hurtful truths & we always affirm ourselves.

We now home-school. We aim to raise free Black people who are never presumed unworthy. We aim to bypass the school to prison pipeline where our children are already systemically & historically set up to fail. We eschew old-school colonial forms of discipline. We recoil at the capitalist oppressions that seep into our humanity. We recognize that many of the institutions where we seek support, in fact, soul-wound our children & youth.

These choices & decisions marginalize us further from mainstream american culture. We struggle. There are few safe spaces for folks like us.

We persist. This is how we humanize.

September, 2018:

We witnessed another traffic stop in our neighborhood.

———

america is amerikkka

amerikkka?
This is amerikkka
dystopia.
My children and I bear witness
to systemic violence
against Black & brown humanity.
A simple brunch outing, just down the street
will make us witness to
       racist systemic violence
police encounters in the name of
       traffic stops
assaulting our Black & brown kin
into fearful submission.
We cry out in dismay
as our children say

Mama, I'm so scared.
Mom, the police are being rough.
He didn't even do anything.
Why are they cuffing him?
Dad, don't take a picture!
Baba, you'll get in trouble, too.
What if they come for you?
Mama, I want to leave here right now.

Child, don't look the other way.
We need to be here.
We can't run from this.
I see your fear.
As I see the fear in the eyes of the stranger cuffed & manhandled
by the police.
Traffic stop.
Child, breathe. Stay calm.
Be ready in case we need to approach the scene.
Child, we are here to witness.
Hold my hand.
Your father is cursing.
Your brother is now in a funk.
Mysteriously, your mother's chronic pain
is searing sharply through her gut.

You know what else I see?
Cafe full of
white folks enjoying their poached eggs
waffles
& sipping their iced tea.
Unstirred.
Unmoved by the scene.
Not one of them bats an eye
as the encounter unfolds.
They do not see
what we see.
They do not bear witness
to trauma by systemic violence.

They sip tea
& fantasize out loud about going to yoga tonight.
No lie.
Child, I can talk to you about the police
racism
systemic violence.
          Traffic stops.
But, I have no words to help you cope
comprehend
or grapple
with white silence
disdain.
apathy
in the face of Black & brown pain.

Be vigilant to avoid owning or misappropriating
Black experiences.

———

Cautionary note to self

Do not collapse brown immigrant status with the real lived
experiences of your Black partner and children. Work
diligently to draw the distinctions. Strive not to overclaim their
experiences as if they were yours.

But, notice when we move through traffic stops & public spaces
as a unit- as a family- their experiences are also yours.

Bettina Love   *Physical & psychological attacks on Black & Brown children's bodies & culture are more than just racist acts...They are the spirit murdering of Black & Brown children...What I am talking about is a slow death, a death of the spirit, a death built on racism & intended to reduce, humiliate & destroy people of color.*

To be american-ish
is to confess
that this land is obsessed
with race.
Racism is the single most pressing
-ism

To be american-ish
is to become desensitized
and dehumanized.

June 25:

Tamir Rice's birthday.

———

Mother of Black Children

Tamir Rice would have celebrated a birthday today.
Antwon Rose at seventeen was laid to rest on this day.
Black lives extinguished
eliminated by a racist system
built on committing the
erasure
& purging
of Black & Indigenous people
&
people of color.
Where is the freedom?
To live? To breathe? To BE?
Last week, we marked Juneteenth.
156+ years of freedom
for Black folks.
Do we celebrate emancipation
while we face annihilation?
I birthed a child
fifteen years ago & named him Freedom.
I beseeched the heavens for a name
befitting a Black brown child born in america.
Freedom! Azad.
"Where is the freedom?"
cry the mothers of all the

Black Indigenous children of color.
How on earth do we birth and raise free children
in a world hell bent on extinguishing
their life force?
On this day,
I embrace all the Mothers
mourning our children's stolen lives as we pray
that one day freedom comes.

*If colonialism is not just about forced occupation of land but
also the mental & emotional oppressions we encounter, then
colonialism is a kind of soul wounding spirit murdering.
Decolonizing is a soulful healing.*

———

***We are not
marginal.
We are
marginalized.
We are People
of the Global
Majority.***

Black folks   Clapping back

Assimilating is to clap to the rhythm of those
around me.
Resisting is to clap back with my own beat.

March, 2019:

*I was called condescending when I corrected someone after they
said NAHmastay.*

———

Bless Your Heart

You call me condescending.
Bless your heart.
I laugh out loud every time somebody calls me that.
But first, I take a deep inhale.
(Om om om)
I take it as a compliment.

Then, I exhale.
(Namaste)

Do I retaliate & call you ignorant?
Let's be real.
I swallow my bile so that I can conceal my hurt.
My self-possession offends you.
Bless your heart.

You call me condescending (& so much more).

Do I call you ignorant?
I dare not.
First, I inhale calm.
Then I exhale poise.
I may not retaliate.
Must bite my tongue & suppress my anger.
I have to own myself while under fire.

I am only condescending in relation to your ignorance.

If I dare shed light on your bias, bigotry,
inform, redirect, or correct you
holding my head high, without centering or coddling you,
I must be arrogant.
I must be condescending.
I dared tell you to do your research & study up.
Educating while brown & other sure is condescending, ain't it?

You say condescending. I say badass.
Namaste.
Bless your heart.

December, 2019:

*When I asked if a desi event was welcoming to my family, the
organizers asked me to explain what I meant.
How do I convey that anti-Blackness can be an energy?*

———

Do we pay attention to where & how anti-Blackness happens? It
is systemic. It is not just in insults or the couched comments, but
also in the energy we radiate, the way we do or do not align our
intentions to ensure the safety of our Black kin. How do we listen
to them? How do we pay attention to them? How do we silence
them or hush them or look the other way? Whose comfort are we
committed to preserving? In the answers to these questions, we
can vibe anti-Blackness or solidarity.

#SayTheirNames

We live in a time when the hashtags proliferate.
The list of names of Black souls lost to racist violence is infinite.
Black lives mattering is still a far-fetched american dream.

No denial.

We wake daily to news of new violence against Black folks. Those with privilege act surprised or feign shock that america is like this. Others flat out deny it & tell us "this is not who we are." If we pay attention, we can tell the truth-that this story is over 500 years old. Black folks are policed & harmed everywhere. From traffic stops to coffee shops to the corner store to schools to streets, can our Black kin go outside or drive or watch birds or sip their coffee in peace?

April, 2018:

Two Black men at a Starbucks in Philadelphia.

───────

Coffee. Black.
No sugar.
I drank a whole pot
alone
sitting in the dark
this rainy Sunday morning
sipping
while I pondered
all the things you can not do
while Black
in america
without getting shot in the back
or shackled

or scorned
or belittled
or dismissed.
Driving while Black
walking while Black
talking on the phone while Black
playing at the park while Black
going to the corner store while Black
giving birth while Black
marching for rights while Black
resting in your own apartment while Black
falling asleep while reading in public while Black
walking across campus to your job while Black.
The list is mighty long, we know.

Who can even breathe while Black?

I drank a whole pot of coffee
no sugar.

In america, can I drink my coffee black
but kin can't even drink coffee while Black?

Poly

I am an american-ish
who grew up on the African continent
spelling color with a u as colour
& splendor as splendour.

I adapted my accents
& my spelling
in the days before spell check.

I am not just polylingual,
I am polycultural.

Even in English, the language,
in which I was schooled,
I switch codes between
southern African
Hinglish
southern american.

spelling BE while Indian

what does it mean to be
class privileged-supposed model-minority-while-always-other
in america?
you could spell
win the Spelling Bee (like a boss)
stand off against another Indian
who spells like a boss, too
either way, we win (or so we think)
for the umpteenth year in a row
you spell like it's your very life that depends on it
you could master the Master's tongue
better than their progeny
you could educate smudge-ucate yourself
up by the bootstraps

like you were told
        you could train to spell
like you were a professional athlete
get those
eyes on the Prize
study study study work work work
& still be
belittled
be dismissed
be invisible
be mocked
we are just kidding they say
joke's on you
your As don't count
study all you want
your win ain't no big deal
you can TRY to win the Bee
but you just can't BE
it's already been decided by the Powers that Be

Code switching

is the mode of linguistic & cultural
survival of those perpetually
stereotyped & othered
in every space we enter.

We learn to adapt & become
shapeshifters in ways that leave
us wondering who or how we truly are.

January, 2019:

They asked me again why I avoid the word diversity.
What is white gaze? Is it a master's tool?

———

Words to signal dominant (white) gaze

Exotic, ethnic, traditional, tribal,
non-white, non-English,
different, diversity,
minority.
Under-represented.

I am not interested in being compared to normative
dominance or met with representation or inclusion into
whiteness.

I now refuse to other myself this way.

August, 2020:

brown american life entails applauding representation
as if it is a revolution.

———

Whose assessments about myself am I taught to value?
Whose opinions and life experiences are devalued?
How do I define my worth?

Bettina Love   *Intersectionality can not be conflated with diversity.*

If "double consciousness" is the internal conflict for colonized or subjugated folks, what does an intersectional consciousness look & feel like?

As an american-ish
I often travel to remote
towns with my Black partner and children,
now youth,
where we enter spaces
that are not open to us.
As we receive stares and glares
for how we dare
enter here,
I know that my survival depends
upon smiling in the face of
white rage and fear.
To be american-ish
is to testify that this land
where you reside
though built on settler colonial genocide
presumes all non-white others
as infringing upon white places and white spaces,
with no accountability
for the history of settler colonial genocide
that bestowed them with this sense of entitlement.

As an american-ish,
people guess I have an accent before I even open my mouth.
As I have perfected my americanisms,
I am often met with raised eyebrows &

"How come you speak without an accent?"

As an american-ish,
I am often compelled
to do the heavy lifting labor
of educating folks
who are white
or white adjacent
& explaining that color blindness is a lethal
form of racism.

Who taught me language?
Who taught me code?
How did I learn the power of language?

W.E.B. Du Bois   *How does it feel to be a problem?*

Vijay Prashad   *What is the karma of brown folk?*

What we are called here:

brown
desi
South Asian
South Asian American

Even if we are seen or represented as a monolith, we contain
multitudes.
We are from Bangladesh, Sri Lanka & Nepal.
They assume we are all Indian.
We are of many castes & faiths.
They assume we are all Hindu.

We are imagined as wealthy, white adjacent, playing tennis at
our homes in the suburbs.
They see doctors, lawyers, professors, not taxi drivers, bodega
workers, dish-washers.
They see & tell a single myth of success.

When I speak of us "desis" or "brown folks," I am hinting at both the collective identity of brown desiness, but also seek to question how our stories are compiled into a single story.

I am learning that when we are unsure about identity, we should ask folks how they would prefer to be identified. Call them by the affiliations they choose rather than place the burdens of external affiliations on them.

Nuance

Our conflicted confounded world
at war with itself
is crying out for nuance.
We the margins
we the marginal,
we see & be all the nuances.
Let us search for nuance,
let us invent new words
& worlds.
I suggest looking at the margins.
When the margins are seen,
when the margins are heard,
nuance lives.

Multiple things are true at the same time.
We ought to normalize simultaneous truths.

———

Audre Lorde   *The true focus of revolutionary change is never merely the oppressive situations that we seek to escape, but that piece of the oppressor which is planted deep within us.*

RESEARCH:

Oppression

systems: white supremacy, patriarchy, caste & capitalism.

institutions: healthcare, education, religion or law enforcement.

impacts: -isms like individualism, colorism, ableism

phobias: xenophobia or Islamophobia.

Let us reveal & talk about our anti-Blackness, a piece of the oppressor planted in us.

Let us consider some of the fraught discussions we brown folks must have.

Those of us who are brown & american are likely to have learned our way through the maze of this place by proximity to whiteness resulting in willful anti-Blackness.
We may be brown or desi or south asian but do we behave like people of whiteness?

When I correct skinfolks on the subtle & blatant ways our anti-Blackness shows up, I am often met with a range of reactions from defensiveness or discomfort to unfriending. Some people describe these behaviors as fragility or gaslighting or reinforcement of privilege. It is all violence.

Let us notice oppressive behaviors we display.

Does brown fragility happen?

I live in the united states in 2021. In these times when Black Lives Matter is a globally understood movement for racial justice, we brown folks are often complicit & fall short of true allyship. We are rarely comrades. I often initiate conversations about race & antiracism with our kin. Most often, I am greeted by the silencing techniques of "chup kar." At other times, especially

with those who enjoy white adjacent privilege, I encounter
the classic playlist known as fragility: denial, gaslighting,
accusation, doubling in, debating & other ways of derailing a
conversation about the truth- that we are guilty of anti-Black
beliefs & behaviors. Scholars debate the veracity of white
fragility. In lived experience, as I name these behaviors, I suspect
that so-called fragility is something we desis have learned from
the colonizers & mastered just as well as our spelling.

Non-Black folks are so immersed in anti-Blackness that we begin
to display the same kinds of guilt-ridden defensiveness, inaction
& fragility as white folks.
Brown fragility happens. Fragility is too misleading a word for
this behavior.

We cannot unlearn our anti-Blackness
unless & until we heal from internalized colonialism
& decolonize.

The notion of fragility is unstable & contested. Is there another more useful word?

―――――

React or reflect?

Here are some of the ways we react when confronted with our oppressive behaviors:
complicit silence, callous indifference, pity, denial, guilt or shame.

When presented with ideas that cause
dissonance or offense,
we are taught to react or overreact.

What if we respond by reflecting instead of reacting
in defense?

How are our activisms duplicitous?

―――――

Chai Tea activism

I hear the outcry of young brown folks
calling out the appropriation of tea
but they rarely speak up to defend Black humanity.
I wonder if there isn't a theatricality
to our duplicitous chai tea
activism.

How is brown-washing harmful?

When my Blindian daughter with her desi first name, African middle name & Black american family name grows up, she is not going to need brown folks to tell her how to say her name or how to be desi or analyze if she is desi enough or at all.

Her diasporic desi mother raised her to love her Black self completely. In a racist world intent on her erasure, she was taught to love & claim herself as Black first & foremost. She has been taught that she is everything & she is who she decides she is. Let us also be clear that her Black kin have embraced her in ways desi misogynoir never can. Could we own up to how desi folks harm biracial Black kin? We cannot demand any performance of singular identity or affiliation from them.

Identity policing is violent. Biracial and multiracial identifications exist.
Erasure is a form of racism.
Stop this bakwaas.

Forcing multi-identified folks to choose only one identity is often how white supremacy operates in identity policing.

Solidarity with our biracial kin requires that we pause and consider how our experiences both intersect and differ.

The desi washing of a Black woman of Indian descent is anti-Black.
Erasing her Blackness in order to self-represent is anti-Black.

Just because she calls on her chittis,
does not mean we get to call her aunty.

To call a Black woman an aunty
is not just insulting but deeply revealing of our internalized
anti-Blackness.

Even our terms of endearment can cause harm if we are not
thoughtful.

Stop the bakwaas | बकवास बंद करो

Black Indians exist.
Black children with desi mothers who proudly identify as Black
do exist.
Erasure of identity and brown-washing of Blackness are forms of
anti-Blackness.

Brown Privilege?

We hold privilege even in a world where we are stereotyped and
oppressed.
When the world is proclaiming that Black Lives Matter, what is
our role?
It is not our role to center ourselves and add harm to Black folks.

Who are we if we are not true in our support for Black humanity?
Who are we when we selectively claim the identity of "person of color" even as we persist in our anti-Blackness?
We have some reckoning to do with our brown privilege.
Brown accountability requires honesty.

There is a way. To center our margins.
There are ways that we can take a seat.
Be quiet, learn & make room for Black & Indigenous folks.

An opportunity comes to me. I ask myself, *Do I take space or make space?*
When I decline & tell the person inviting me that instead of taking space, I'd like to nominate a phenomenal younger Black woman, he is flabbergasted.

Why?

He's never met a non-Black African who did this.
Fellow brown folks, we have a lot of work to do.
Let us make space instead of hoarding it.

Our silence & silencing of other marginalized folks is often how we perpetuate white supremacy. If we are folks of color staying silent about racism or Islamophobia or transphobia or any oppression in our midst, we uphold the here & now.

We are complicit.

I said it out loud. I put it on paper.
White supremacy uses us brown folks as tools to perpetuate itself.

When will we do our part to dismantle white supremacy?

I know we were taught to be nervous about words like this & skittish about allegations of racism. I say that it is time to use these words openly.

Hurt people hurt people?

It would sadden me if you concluded from these pages that we desis are exclusively harmful. I tell the truth as I have witnessed it. I do this to lay bare my heart wounds & be held accountable for ways we all harm.

It is said, hurt people hurt people. We do.
Healing people heal people, too.

These conversations about our own oppressions are often raw, imperfect & discomforting. Many of us avoid them. So few of us are able to muster up the needed vulnerability to show up to them. They are so vital.

―――

Disrupting bakwaas

What might it look like for brown desi folks to be disruptors? What if instead of rushing to defend ourselves–saying not all of us are harmful or not all of us are anti-Black–we own up to all the ways we hold up the systems & behaviors of anti-Blackness? What if we chose to disrupt them?

They tell me that not every oppressive behavior is racist. This is true. It is also true that racism is often at the root of much oppression.

———

Luke Wood/Frank Harris III   *Race lighting*

Racism is violent.
It is not merely fragile privilege.
It is not an unintentional mistake.
It is often not micro.
It is not a harmless comment.
It is systemic. It is structural. It is personal.
It is violent. It is unjust.

Misnaming or minimizing racism is a form or racial gaslighting.

Gayatri Sethi

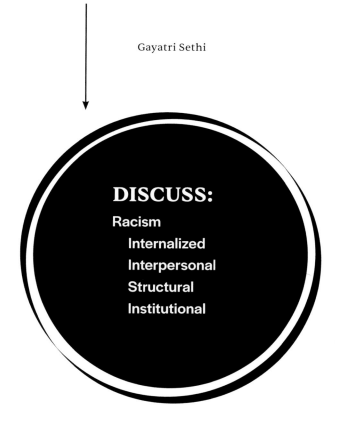

DISCUSS:

Racism
    Internalized
    Interpersonal
    Structural
    Institutional

Race is socially constructed but materially real. Racism is also a system that determines access, privilege & power.
Blackness & brownness are constructed in relation to whiteness.
An invitation: Let us read up, unlearn, and learn.

How do brown folks defend whiteness?

September, 2019:

Canadadian Prime Minister "More Enthusiastic About Costumes Than Is Sometimes Appropriate"

———

Let us say someone who performs allyship messes up. What if they dress up in brownface for a party? Whose side do we take? Do we excuse or do we stand up for ourselves?

We might attack our skinfolk to defend a privileged white man who isn't as "for brown people" as he claims to be. Do we tell the truth? He is fundamentally a white racist. Or, do we hold him as an exception?
Exceptionalism, like tokenism, is dangerous racism.
It masquerades as one thing while it stings like another.
Let us learn that attacking each other is enacting the colonizer mentality ingrained in us.
We cannot.
Most importantly, watch how quickly we degenerate into anti-Blackness over any discourse like this because we have been slipping & sliding & refusing to believe our Black kin who warned us not to align with whiteness.
Black people have been telling us & we don't heed their warnings.
It's time for brown folks to stop erasing ourselves to uphold the status-quo.
We cosign harm when we stand by in silence.
Stop the bakwaas.

DISCUSS:
Oppression olympics
Performative allyship
Woke washing
Slacktivism

Oppressive behaviors seem to always cut & wound deeper when they are inflicted by folks who share identities with us.

What is the karma of brown folk in settler colonialism?

Bury the model minority myth.
Refuse to be a weapon against Black america.
Refuse to erase Indigenous truths.
Refuse to ally with whiteness.
Pay the price of refusal.

bell hooks   *White supremacy is a useful term for understanding the complicity of people of color in upholding and maintaining racial hierarchies that do not involve force (i.e. slavery, apartheid).*

This truth means that we do not have to be white to exercise white supremacist control over Black people.
Let me say this another way. We can be oppressed but still uphold systems of oppression.

Danielle Slaughter   Caping & gatekeeping for white supremacy

The truth is that non-Black folks like me cape for white supremacy.
We protect white innocence.
We are white adjacent.
We are agents
of white supremacy.

Whether in our workplaces
or hidden spaces,
do we ally with whiteness
or support our Black kin?

I will never know what certain experiences entail, so I do not seek to speak "for" or on behalf of anyone. I lay bare my own precarious predicaments.

Rules of engagement

There is a deeply felt violence known as disowning that traumatizes many of us who venture outside desi heteronormative rules of marriage.

We come to know intimately what unbelonging means.

We are shunned & held up as examples to deter others from following suit. Even in the West, where interracial marriage is often accepted, desi folks rarely marry outside their race or caste, and those who do often marry white partners. There are too many hushed rules of engagement & far too many traumatic consequences as deterrents. It is also true that interracial marriage is not proof that we are not racist.

Desis love their tennis. We tolerate white men's tantrums on the court & in board rooms, but when a Black athlete shows emotion to stand up for herself, the commentary is toxic.

———

Desi Misogynoir

Brown people who watch tennis and have commentary, here are a few words I wish to convey:
We need to unlearn misogynistic anti-Blackness.
If we find ourselves describing Serena's behavior as a "tantrum" or policing her behaviors or tone by saying she was "rude" or "unprofessional" or accuse her of poor sportsmanship—

If we find ourselves commenting on her actions without understanding that what occurred is systemic, deliberate & absolutely unjust—

We must reflect upon our own misogynoir.

This is the word Dr. Moya Bailey uses to describe the specific way racism and misogyny combine to oppress Black women.

Reflect:
When was the last time I described desi relatives & spouses the way I describe Black women?

When was the last time I defied the patriarchy implicit in my upbringing?

When have I stood up for myself when a man did me wrong?

In public? On a global stage?
Yaar, take a look in the mirror.
We see an instance of a wronged Black woman standing up for
herself
and take it out of the context
of her daily struggles
& the relentless
racism & sexism she encounters
every day
everywhere.

We call her names & vilify her
when we ought to advocate for & venerate her.
If you find yourself aligning with all the whiteness or
defending the status-quo,
if you find yourself tone policing or otherwise replicating
harmful commentary
that adds to the systemic harms of
Black women & trans folks everywhere—
Stop your misogynoir.

*I mess up so often. Deeply rooted oppressive behaviors rise to
the surface. I feel guilt or shame; those feelings paralyze me into
inaction. What do I do when I realize my mistake?*

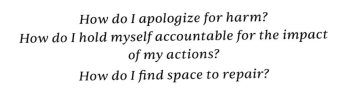

How do I apologize for harm?
How do I hold myself accountable for the impact of my actions?
How do I find space to repair?

To be desi-ish african-ish american-ish
is to revere your own mythic goddesses
while you offer deep bows to the
humans
who are rarely respected by desis.
To be american-ish desi-ish
is to call out our (not so) secret biases
& prejudices.
When the desis in america
wish silent complicity,
I speak out.
To be desi-ish & american-ish
is to refuse to make excuses for your kin
who uphold anti-Black oppressions
when we ought to dismantle the
systems that oppress us all.

In my american-ish
existence,
I am often questioned & asked
why I affiliate consistently with Black folks.
It is implied that this is a form of reverse racism.

To be me
is to understand the unspoken
that immigrants often adapt
to white adjacent forms of success.
I chose to align myself with my lived truths.
I decided to be an immigrant who says out loud
Black Lives Matter.

Interrupting dominant whiteness is a strategy for anti-oppression.

September 21:

*#chaiday? Capitalism invents holidays
that promote cultural appropriation.*

———

#NationalChaiDay

I'm a desi who rarely drinks chai.

Chai tastes of colonialism to me.
Do we imbibe high tea?
Drink it like the British or French?
Raise our pinkies & tickle our fancies?
I reject the colonial appropriations of chai.
A therapeutic desi ritual is now bereft.
I find no joy in chai.
I serve it to guests & leave my cup empty.

Chai tastes of patriarchy to me.
All the times I was commanded, "Beti, chai lao" or "chai pilao"
have made me bitter towards tea.

I wish I could've said "nah."
"Make the chai your own damn self.
You didn't birth me so I could be your personal chai-on-demand maker.
Ask my bhai to make you chai."

The one time I refused the request, I learned to swallow my defiance & make tea in compliance.
Chai tastes of patriarchy to me.

And now when a gori barista serves up whitewashed milky froth as chai, I gag.
This is what cultural appropriation tastes like.
I choose bottomless coffee, though bitter.
It tastes of defiance to me.
My occasional chai is a very bittersweet indulgence.

I notice how many social justice terms are appropriated or weaponized.

———

On cultural appropriation

How I break it down with a ten-year-old:

When in doubt, do not.

No. If your ancestors are white colonizers, know it's a big no to you.

Do not consume.
No. Sacred items aren't costumes.
No. We can't just wear things from cultures we haven't studied or learned about.
No. We can't wear or use Indigenous items even if our great-grandfather had a First Nations parent.
No. If it's "just dress up" & superficial, it's not for us.
Do not sell what's not ours.

No. We can't profit from cultural arts or practices of
marginalized peoples.

Do not assume.
No. Stop & think it through.
No. Even if we are people of color, we can't just take or wear or
practice without learning first.
No. It's not a free for all.
No. If we have a shadow of a doubt, assume we can not.

Yes, be mindful.
Yes, we can learn about our own heritages & learn to be proud of
them.
Yes, we practice cultural appreciation by learning from each
other.
Yes, we partake in cultural exchanges when we are invited.
Yes, we are one human family.
Yes, we are distinct cultures & peoples.
Yes, be culturally humble.

Do not ever take what's not offered to you.

When in doubt, do not.

*I wanted to practice yoga again. But, then I recalled that here,
yoga means to have your own ancestral practices
stolen or appropriated without care & then hurled back at you
through capitalism. How do I explain to whiteness the casteism
in yoga?*

———

Nah to white Yoga

I break out in hives when I enter
white studio spaces
where whiteness has stolen
my ancestral practices
whitewashed them
& sold them back to me diluted & poisoned
with privilege
entitlement
& callousness.

I am the brown desi-ish
who will no longer stand by
as westerners appropriate
my ancestral inheritance
& claim to "Nama-slay"
while sipping beer
doing poses in breweries
sometimes with cats and goats.

This is not yoga.
I say Nah-mastay.
Nah, you may not use or appropriate my ancestral ways.

Try telling privileged folks that they may not have something?
I am told I am a hater who is not spiritually elevated
enough to practice yoga.

I offer a deal
that might heal.
Learn to love brown people like me
as much as you claim to love your studio yoga.
Leave the beer at the brewery.
Leave the goats on the farm.
Do no harm.
Bow down in genuine humility
downward dog to brown humans
& call it movement.
Leave the yoga to the yogis.
No more white yoga.

Namaste. | नमस्ते

March, 2020:

*Women's History Month. I forgive past me for having been so
enamored with what I later realized was just white feminism.*

———

Nah to white feminism | नही

I used to study feminism. I used to teach feminisms. In this
field of study, I learned that white feminism protects whiteness.
It does not uplift brown, Indigenous & Black folks. If white
feminism gatekeeps for white supremacy, it is not feminism at
all. The womanism of Black feminists liberates all of humanity.
When Black folks are free, we are all free.
I say nah to white feminism.

Refusal

What does refusal to align with whiteness culture look like?
For me, it is to say nah to all the ways that my culture, identity &
spirit are consumed.
I do not consent to my own consumption.
Refusal feels like unbelonging,
But it is freeing.

To be american-ish
is to be the brown desi-ish
mother of Black children.
This demands that you
unlearn a lot of what
you were taught
about respectability politics.
To be american-ish
is to realize
that there is an unspoken
expectation
to conform, adapt & assimilate.
Refusing to do so
comes at tremendous risk.

The other day, I confessed to someone that I was tired of living brown otherness in america. They retorted, "be grateful. You get to live here. Immigrants should be grateful instead of tired."

Ungrateful Immigrant

I am called an ungrateful immigrant.
because I do not celebrate america.

They say I am anti-patriotic.
Why are you even here?
Go back where you came from.

america has never loved
the Indigenous
the enslaved & their descendents
the brown
the immigrants
the Muslims
or the LGBTQ+

Us
the marginalized
the terrorized
the invisible & erased
who make america

america
has always been an imperial
state perpetrating genocide.
Peddling superiority & promises of
freedoms.
Lies masking oppressions manifold.
To speak these truths
is to be told
you are unwelcome here.

We already knew
but we are here anyway.
Telling truth & resisting injustice
are the ultimate patriotism.
Didn't you know?
We know.

Folks pity us. What is that about? Is pity not a form of superiority?
Is superiority not supremacy?

———

Truthful reckoning

This is a truth that I need to contend with:
we, the othered, are guilty of self-othering
to meet white gaze.
When I realize this,
I refuse to self-exoticise.

Whiteness is addicted to consuming
the pain & trauma of brown others.
It feeds off our grief & mourning.

I refuse to be used to satisfy
the insatiable appetite for our pain.
I often refuse access to my trauma.

Instead, I offer myself as evidence of our resilience.

White gaze, like buri nazar, harms & distorts my being.

———

Immigrant confessions

Those of us taught by colonized education to stay on a narrow path to acceptability, respectability & success often confuse systemic inequities with personal failures. Where unjust systems meet personal growth, I pitch an unwieldy tent. I dwell there.

They said, "Aunty, imposterism is so real." I countered, "Is it, though?"

———

Imposterism

If the yardstick to measure your worth
is cisheternonomative and white,
but you are oh so "other"...

If the standards of success are set by white supremacy...
If your intelligence is measured in relation
to whiteness
or maleness
or cis-genderedness...

If you step back and see
that the rules,
meters
& metrics that you're measuring yourself by are all
inventions for oppression...

You ask for an inch tape and say nay to the yardstick
designed to keep you doubting & second-guessing
yourself.

These measures are invented to demean and depress
you.

Let us tell this truth:
you ain't no imposter!

You got a syndrome for real, though.
It is called oppression.
Next time you feel like an imposter,
ask yourself if it's not oppression.

You are so much more than enough.

Reframe:

The systems of oppression & exclusion are the ultimate
imposters.

Are we always too much & not enough, too? Who decided I was competent, clever or qualified? How did they evaluate or assess me?

———

master's tools

Perfection is a master's tool.
Who taught me perfection?
Who expected my perfection?
Comparison is a master's tool.
Criticism is a master's tool.
Conflict avoidance is a master's tool.
Silence is a master's tool.

Fight fire with fire

They say: Do not fight fire with fire.
Ally Henny   I reply: Our fire for liberation from oppression
is not the same fire of oppressive hate.
Our fires are not the same.

How much elitism did I pick up under the guise of education?

———

about me: more specifics

I hold a PhD in Comparative Education from an elite university. I used to insist folks inclined to undervalue or dismiss my worth address me by the title I earned: Dr. Sethi.

I spent more than two decades being a professor, instructor & academic advisor. I was gifted at instructing. I felt at home in the classroom & knew its rhythms as if my instinct to teach had been passed down to me by invisible forces.

When I was forced to reckon with the so-called glass ceiling & systemic inequities that made it near impossible for me to survive in academia, I wondered if I had failed.

I doubted my own abilities instead of recognizing the unjust ways in which my gender & identity as an immigrant precluded me from climbing the ladder to tenure.

I stepped off the conventional academic path, chose a circuitous way around teaching to transgress, all the while wondering when academia would "diversify" enough to make space for me.

It hasn't. I am not waiting.

I no longer use this title or uphold the elitism that often surfaces when we are asked "what we do." I now measure my worth in new ways I have yet to articulate.

When asked about my professorial life, I say: If I am not using the title, educational privilege & knowledge I accumulated to uplift & serve others, it is of no value at all.

RESEARCH:

Forms of decolonization
Meanings of decolonization
The memefication of decolonization

April 2019:

French billionaires pledge 300 million euros to rebuild the Notre Dame. The world mourns its ashes.

——

Future dreams

I envision a day
when 300 million of any currency
will be raised in under a day
by colonizers
as reparations
to restore the rightful dues of
the Indigenous and the colonized.
I dream of a day when 300 million
will be spent in under a day as restoration
by colonizers
to recreate the pillaged and stolen
     artifacts
     histories
     gifts
of the formerly colonized.
Those millions would be wiser invested
in reparations
to a future civilization
than restoration
of symbols of old.

Decolonizing is unsettling.

———

How do I decolonize?

I no longer center the dominant narratives or narrators.
Inch by inch, moment by moment,
breath by breath, I center the margins.
I center myself & my soul.

This is how I decolonize.

An invitation to spoken word:
Read the following aloud.
Imagine all the meanings of the words allowed.

Decolonize your grocery cart.
Decolonize your sexual preferences.
Decolonize your medicine cabinet.
Decolonize your therapy.
Decolonize your worship.

Decolonize your schooling.
Decolonize your reading lists.
Decolonize your citations.
Decolonize your media diet.
Decolonize your garbage.
Decolonize your time.

Decolonize your capitalist consumption.
Decolonize & de-ionize materialism.
Decolonize your holidays.
Decolonize sacred symbols.
Decolonize your partnerships.
Decolonize your friendships.
Decolonize your parenting.

Decolonize your spirit.
Decolonize your mind.
Decolonize your life.

Decolonize every damn thing.

Indigenize. Humanize.

*I have no
idea what my indigeneity
might even look like.*

———

Reverse Racism?

Am I reverse racist
because I have committed
to an antiracist life?
Am I reverse racist
because I seek to
center Black lives?

Reverse racism is a figment of the white imagination
that sees in a disavowal from white gaze & approval
an abrogation, not a liberation.
When we decolonize, we center the margins.
In america, this means we center Black & Indigenous folks.

*Is white gaze not buri nazar? How can nazar be a culturally
sustaining way to learn & teach about white gaze?*

——

Nazar | نظر | नज़र

I refuse white gaze.
Refusal of white gaze will cost us.
It will also free us.

Mantra for karma reckoning | मंत्र कर्म

Internalized oppression is real.
Internalized oppression is really real.
Internalized oppression is really oppressive.

Octavia Butler   *In order to rise from its own ashes, a phoenix first must burn.*

An affirmation for truth

Antiracism in heart work.

call to activism

Center the margins, comrades.
                    Center ourselves.

an american observation:
We live in a time of macro gaslighting.

Protestors are called terrorists.
Settlers are called citizens.
Terrorists are called protestors.
Nationalists are patriots.
Compatriots are anti-nationalists.

We live in a time of macro gaslighting.

July, 2020:

I notice that even the self-professed allies & those who claim to be woke often demand unity before justice & love without accountability.

———

How to be a desi-ish Antiracist?

I realize that by virtue of growing up on the African continent, I learned a distinct way of seeing the world that centers Black joy, resilience, beauty & glory. Blackness was normative in an expansive sense.

Even today on american soil, my children very rarely encounter this celebration of Blackness.

On my lifelong antiracism journey (some of which I have detailed in these pages), I have come to understand that my role is to continue learning, be humble & amplify Black excellence in its abundant forms. I do this in intimate settings such as my poems, teaching & community building with like-hearted people. I grew up in the Bahá'í faith & this spiritual community taught me the importance of social justice. Many of our teachings center on the oneness of humanity, unity of religions, racial harmony & the equality of genders. That foundational orientation, set early in childhood, along with my upbringing in southern Africa have prepared me to see that one of my responsibilities is to be a racism interruptor.

I am an injustice interrupter because I am well versed in unbelonging.

I often wonder how I might put my body, voice & extensive knowledge in the way of harm against my Black kin. I have a role & responsibility to be antiracist & many of the verses that speak out & call out the -isms in my communities are intended as disruptive forms of collective care.
Is it not loving to tell the truth in the service of justice?

Conversations are vital. They are a start.
They are not enough.

iii. REVOLUTIONS

Does unlearning oppressive behaviors come before or after solidarity?

The language of liberation

One of the realities of my life here in the sacred lands of the Muscogee is that I have accrued significant cultural capital. This educational privilege means that I can speak as fluently in the words of whiteness or academia as I can in the words of my mother's tongue. Sometimes, I speak academic lingo more fluently than words of affection or care. There is an alienation in this reality. One outcome is that it is here that I have learned the language of feminisms, critical race theories & abolition, too. I have learned to unlearn ableist language & relearn words that are more encompassing or inclusive. I have witnessed the power of words that alienate & phrases that signal sanctuary.

Aliyekupanidisha simpige teke. Do not kick the one who helped you up. Why look down on your humble origins?

———

Cynthia Foronda **Cultural humility | ਨਿਮਰਤਾ**

What might it mean to practice cultural humility towards Black folks?
At home in Gaborone, cultural humility would mean declining the oppressive practices, taught by colonizers, of treating all Black Africans as "servants." When brown & white Africans act like the bosses of all Black folks, a part of me screams out loud about this humiliation. Where is the humility towards the keepers of this land we inhabit? At home in Decatur, sacred lands of the Muscogee Creek, cultural humility would mean learning the true history of america.

Cultural humility would mean that we non-Black folks unlearn the colonizer ways of divide & conquer. We would refuse to be model minorities who benefit from the subjugation of Black folks.

Cultural humility would mean that we do not take space. Cultural humility means that we unlearn the white adjacent ways we have adopted.

Cultural humility invites us to relearn how to center the stories & narratives & histories of folks who built this land with unfathomable resourcefulness despite enslavement and ongoing systemic injustice.

Cultural humility means to abstain from employing the catchall category "people of color" selectively in ways that erase Black folks.

Cultural humility opens doors instead of gatekeeping.

Cultural humility is to own up to ways we are complicit in the erasure of & systemic violence towards Black lives. Cultural humility requires that we refuse to be color-blind.

Cultural humility is to know without a shadow of a doubt that we can never fully know what it means to be raced Black in america.

Cultural humility is to honor and compensate the labor of Black folks.

Cultural humility is to see that there are as many ways to be Black as there are stars in the night sky.

Cultural humility makes way for us to be actively antiracist instead of passively non-racist.

In essence, cultural humility is akin to a deep spiritual practice in which we, non-Black folks, recenter the humanity, resilience & power of Black folks. It is a stance of opening ourselves to learning, unlearning & relearning.

Cultural humility is a prerequisite to solidarity.

What am I trying to fit into?
Why is belonging often forced or required?

───

Dismantling is unbelonging

Those who refuse to cower
or center the comfort of those in power
must become comfortable being villainized,
removed & disdained.

Dismantling systemic oppression is a commitment to
unbelonging.

Is it possible that the need to belong & the policing of belonging
are forms of internalized oppression?
Could it be that a path to being free is rooting in our own
heritage even as we get free from belonging?

Who taught me liberation?
Who taught me revolution?
How do we dream up solidarity?

I was taught to venerate & thank teachers.

———

Who taught me liberation?
Black folks. Black feminists. Black scholars.
Black creatives. Black artists. Black activists.
Black friends. Black chosen family. Black community.

It is a truth to honor that Black women's liberation
includes us all.

Identity politics can be revolutionary

It is a lie taught to us that identity politics is divisive or
separatist.

Create a politics that is aligned with our own
experiences.

Combahee River Collective	*We realize that the liberation of all oppressed peoples necessitates the destruction of the political-economic systems of capitalism and imperialism as well as patriarchy.*

Identity policing is soul wounding

Those who police our identities
with their words & attitudes & rules & policies
soul wound us.
No matter their intentions, this is the impact.

Soul?

That part of us connected to both our divinity and humanity.

August 5, 2019:

Toni Morrison passes away. I notice that people of all races co-opt the grief of my Black kin as they whitewash her legacy.

———

I'd like to offer my deepest condolences to all my Black friends & family mourning the passing of Toni Morrison. She is your Ms. Morrison. She is your ancestor now.

I remind us non-Black folks not to center ourselves or appropriate emotions that are not ours to claim.

She was bluntly clear: in everything she wrote & taught, she said she wrote for & to Black folks.
I'm grateful that I learned I was on sacred ground reading

Beloved or The *Bluest Eye* as a brown immigrant child arriving in america with very little understanding of the racist history & dynamics I entered.

I read her books. I learned.

She wasn't writing for me, yet I benefited from her words. Even in her passing, she taught me not to claim or appropriate Black grief.

I am learning that Black grief is sacred.

As I grieve the passing of an intellectual giant & an extraordinary human I deeply admire, I remember that she taught me that Black stories are Black stories.

She taught me that I'm welcome to read these stories & be uplifted by them, but they were not written for me. It's appropriate that I honor her by remembering that she taught us not to appropriate Black folks' experiences or feelings even as we teach & learn about them.

I honor her by practicing cultural humility towards Black folks. Deep bow.

I am learning that antiracism is boundary work. I am learning to center Black stories & truths even as I tell my own. I must be mindful to honor boundaries without overstepping.

Nod to Black feminists, activists, & abolitionists

Maya Angelou, Audre Lorde, bell hooks, Toni Morrison & Ntozake Shange.
Brittney Cooper. Emily Caruthers. Adrienne Maree Brown.
Moya Bailey. Kimberlé Crenshaw.
Angela Davis. Mariame Kaba. Bettina Love.
My students, friends & sistren.

Black feminists are my intellectual influencers.
I listen to their teachings & their feelings.
I witness the truths that my colonial education
hid from me.

I vow to do better.

Maya Angelou   *Do the best you can until you know better. Then when you know better, do better.*

bell hooks says, *The margin is more than a site of deprivation. It is also the site of radical possibility, a space of resistance... a site one stays in, clings to even, because it nourishes one's capacity to resist. It offers to one the possibility of radical perspective from which to see and create, to imagine alternatives, new worlds.*

Kimberlé Crenshaw teaches us intersectionality-how our identities and oppressions-overlap.

Gloria Anzaldua tells us, *Caminante, no hay puentes, se hace puentes al andar.*

Audre Lorde cautions, *If I didn't define myself for myself, I would be crunched into other people's fantasies for me and eaten alive.*

> In these liberatory words,
> I feel seen.
> I have a place.
> I imagine possibility.
> I practice creativity.
> I own the margins.
> I build bridges there.

bell hooks taught me

I witnessed bell hooks read from her work & exude her wisdom. I was never the same.

I mustered up my courage to approach & thank her. As she signed my book with words affirming radical love, she asked my name.

The next time I saw her read from her work, she said she remembered me by name.

This gift to be seen & remembered by someone as magnetic as bell hooks transformed me. Did she know I was struggling to reconcile the white feminisms of my graduate school training with my heartfelt commitment to liberating myself & folks of color just like me?

She might have seen it. She might even have known it. After all, she walked & studied in the same halls & libraries where we met.

On the day I met bell hooks again, I remembered myself.

In those few moments, she taught me more than the learned professors & advisors who examined & interrogated my work & worth.

This memory of bell hooks & her words guide me often during days when I am lost.

Audre Lorde   *Revolution is not a one-time event. Without community, there is no liberation.*

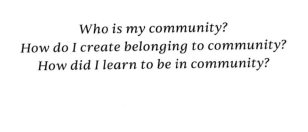

Who is my community?
How do I create belonging to community?
How did I learn to be in community?

October 27, 2018:

Ntozake Shange passes away. My Black kin are grieving. Folks remind us to give people their flowers while they are here. I learn that she, like my elders, had dementia. Did she receive her flowers?

—

I have lost many people & I have suffered deep regret.
In the time of coronavirus, I could not be with my chosen family
who passed away.

I write this for all the folks I did not thank enough while they
were still with us.

Beloved,

did you know how much we loved you?

As you fought to catch your breath
could not speak
could not even write
when you battled to hold on to life,
Did you know how much
we'd mourn your
passing?

Did we show you love while you were among the living?

I suspect we did not.
I suspect that you
flew from this earthly plane
relying on the Love you found within.

Cautionary note: I have no words to convey the need for nuance when speaking of Black folks. There are so many toxic tropes that constrain their humanity. If I am not careful, I might slip & harm them even as I try to thank them.

———

Asante tupu haijai chungu. Empty thanks do not fill the pot.

Debt of Love to Black women

I owe radical love to Black women.

Who taught me to love myself?

Many women
(it breaks me to confess)
taught me to see women with
eyes of jealousy and gossip
my own women taught me
to speak of myself to myself
in words of self-deprecation
never satisfaction.
My own women
(it hurts me to realize)
taught me
to beat myself up
to put myself away
to suit the comfort of others.

My own taught me
to hide myself behind
expectations and responsibility.

Who taught me to love myself?

Black feminists.
Audre Lorde
bell hooks
Maya Angelou
Toni Morrison.
Their words were balms
a soothing kind of liberation.
The more I read them,
the more my sore self
wounded by precarious sense of self
uplifted my self
by speaking to myself
with gentle care pyar.
They inspire my inclination
for affirmation.

Even as I cite & offer credit to the people who have taught me, I realize that it is an unjust predicament that Black folks guide us even as we harm them.

———

Black feminists taught me

I learned to let go of those
inner critics.
The brown voices of comparison
that thrive on keeping me cowering
to the male gaze as I navigate the patriarchal maze.

It was Black women friends
who smiled at me with their eyes
& threw compliments like confetti my way.

How could it be that they see me?
They see me.
So they teach me
their stances & their dances
their words & their breaths

teach me:
love yourself like you're magic
no matter if nobody else does.
My eyes water from the shine
of the truth that if there's any one thing
Black women teach me daily
it's that we survive by loving ourselves
when nobody else does.

It was & is Black Women
the sisters, the professors, the writers
the nieces, the students, the friends
who saw me with genuine admiration

who taught me to shed
the self-criticism
the harshness
the never enoughness.

If they saw me with eyes of love,
maybe I'd be worthy & grow into it.

I birthed a daughter
who teaches me daily
how to wrap myself tight
with I love you
embraces
that are infinite & long.
Her arms wrap round & round
I whisper to her,
"Divine made you so
beautiful. Love yourself."
I see the circle.

Rachel Ricketts *What if instead of exacerbating the systemic burnout of Black women, I did my part to alleviate it?*

Grace & hope

My mother by marriage taught me to say grace at the meals we shared.
She would say, bless this food for the nourishment of our bodies.
Amen.
She would say, keep hope alive,
like Jesse said. But, he got it from the Bible.
Amen.

I would leave her home & presence filled with stories of her ancestors, memories of her younger years.
I was fueled by a keen awareness that it is through her grace that my family is possible.

Our home

This home we are building is a fortress of well-being.
We leave our shoes at the door. We wash our hands first thing.
When we enter, there is light & a faint hint of cumin in the air.
We eat on fading table cloths purchased long ago from Victoria Falls.
We are surrounded by treasures in peacock designs from Delhi.
Our books are piled throughout the house.
We are always reminded of our family all over the world.
It is always Black History Month over here.
The aroma or fresh lit incense & coffee brewing wakes us.
We listen to jazz with baba & the beats of bhangra with mama.
Any given Saturday, we might hear kirtan intermingled with Farsi chants of Bahá'í prayers.

On Sundays, we Whatsapp Nani and sometimes Mamu, too.
We eat pakoras with chai on rainy days.
We crave mama's daal when we need comfort.
We hear Hindi, Spanish & Setswana.
We dream of Botswana night skies.
We speak the language of virtues & translate the boli of justice.
We pray our home is a sanctuary.

Does america love Black people?

I ask my beloved after he reflects on his father's passing from
lung cancer all too soon. He was a veteran twice over who loved
his country enough to go to two wars for it. I ask if america loved
him when he worked at the post office or sought treatment for
his cancer. My beloved and I muse that america loves Black
culture and Black icons. america loves the Obamas and Oprah.
america loves the exceptions & the exceptional. america loves to
consume Blackness, but does this mean that america loves
Black people?

Pyar Revolution

Once I learn to love myself,
it is a revolution.
Love yourself
even if nobody loves you.

My pyar encompasses my people, my batho.

What does it mean to be a Bahá'í ?

We often reply that to be a Bahá'í simply means to love all the world. Abdu'l-Baha's words are repeated: "to love humanity and try to serve it; to work for universal peace and universal brotherhood."

These principles have been the rhythms of my life.

I am deeply distrusting of nationalism & patriotism. I participate in my own unbelonging by refusing to become a naturalized U.S. citizen, choosing precarity in the form of permanent residence applications that are subject to expiration. I also refuse to own property in the sacred lands where I reside.

The language of prayers & holy writings is imprinted deeply into my being. This faith is the spiritual source of my lifelong commitment to social justice & well-being. Even so, like many faith or spiritual communities, these spaces are often where our soul wounds are opened rather than healed.

What does ethical & spiritual fortitude require of me?
Steadfast integrity.

———

Pyar to my Beti

Beloved child of mine,

be fierce in the face of injustice.

Do not cower in the face of unfairness.
Stand up to it.
Use your voice.
Raise your words to stand up for yourself.
If the world calls you shaming names,
so be it.
They can call you whatever they want, but you already know who
you are.
Stand courageous-true to your name-in your truths.

You have the powers and strengths of ancestral goddesses in you.
You are a descendent of Kali. Shakti.
You are a descendent of Oshun, Inna & Ala.

Be fierce & fearless.
Be like Kali, destroying the oppressions.
They will call you kali for your skin tone & Blackness.
They might try to shame you into subservience.
They might try to discipline you into obedience.
They might frustrate you into rageful tears.

Be like Ala, Earth goddess to the Igbo
for whom candles are lit,
altars are dusted off,
yam feasts and festivals are held

& dances are danced
to cleanse away
ward off
old energies
of racism & sexism.

A recurring reminder to my beti: you need not perform any
identity. You need not be anyone but yourself. You are blessed
with an Igbo middle name. Akanya, warrior bringer of harmony.

———

Humanity of Black folks

If we aim to shift the tides, we unlearn our bakwaas &
relearn ways to engage with Black folks.
What does it mean to dignify our kin?
Sometimes, deifying & putting Black folks on pedestals
robs them of their humanity.
I hear my kin warn against this kind of tokenizing &
I seek for ways to offer respect to those whom racism
robs of humanity. They show me that it is not their job to
teach me. Even as they are harmed by oppression, they
are often expected to save us from our own ignorance.
This life of expectation & the tropes of "strong Black
people" have exhausted or harmed them. They say again
& again: we are so tired. Save the saviorism.

Austin
Channing
Brown
How can we dignify humanity?
What is our sacred responsibility for reciprocity?

How do we honor the endurance & resilience & trauma of our Black kin without denying their humanity?

A note to self when they call you difficult:

I am difficult. Je suis compliquée.
I neither confirm nor deny this. I am attracted to difficulty.
I chuckle in self-recognition when I am accused of complicating or overthinking everything.
I even have a "difficult name."
Log & relatives berate me for being difficult. They tell me I do not let things go. I do not let slight slights slide. I do not play along with lies. I do not overlook intended insults. I rarely choose to play along to get along. I choose to be difficult. I am a thorn in your proverbial side. I call out bakwaas foolishness. I call in the hurtful bigotry.
After all, I am definitely attracted to difficulty.
Je suis vraiment compliquée.

I am learning to be unapologetic.

An amusing musing

In many cultures throughout time, women like me have been accused of witchcraft.
When I have been accused of being a chudail, I claim to be a jadoogarni.
When I am accused of witchy ways, I glow with magic.

Stepmother

I am a stepmother. In all the cultures I have been socialized in, this identity is rarely positive. We are assumed to be evil. I brave these tropes as I create new ways to be a parent to the children of my heart & their children, too. Thank heavens, I learned that kinship is forged by motho among batho.

Together Family │ खानदान

Realizing that dunya looks down upon my interracial family, I have done my utmost to guard my family tenderly. I rarely share pictures of the youth or our family outside our trusted circle. Log are likely to call our pictures beautiful, but how rarely do they truly see us in our fullness.

Interracial marriages & mixed race children are not proof that racism is over. I often wonder when we will see & understand the depths of care & intention required to be in family across races. Many of us fall apart from the relentless fractures & oppressions.

Are there any trauma-free humans walking this earth?

———

Immigrant narratives are often trauma stories

Roxane Gay asks
how do we write trauma?

Before I read her thoughtful essay, I jot down:
Slowly. Mindfully. Tenderly. Compassionately.

For me, writing potentially traumatic experiences of
unbelonging requires keeping things general & vague. I refuse
to regurgitate every slap in the face or instance of discrimation.
Some psychologists say that retelling trauma creates more
trauma. Often, we repeat the cycles instead of interrupting them.
I write my trauma vaguely, slowly, cautiously.
This is my trauma writing response.

Trauma response

Hiding identities can be a trauma response to othering &
oppression. When some of your identities conflict with each
other, then you adapt and hide them to get by. But when this
becomes a way of life, a forgetting of sorts, you lose vital parts
of your selves. How do you recoup your lost selves? Or, do you go
adrift?

Revolt | ਰੇਵਲੁਸ਼ਨ

The jolt to revolt
is a spark that turns into a flame
to burn down oppressive ways.

Hopeful audacity

Jesse Jackson

What does hope look like?

Some days, hope is driving your children to their
cello lesson.

These days, hope is double masking to meet a
relative six feet apart.

Hope is interfaith kinship & chosen family
bonds.

What does hope feel like?

Hope feels like a walk in the winter rain to visit
Mom's resting place on her birthday.

Like teaching.

Like writing & creating.

Hope feels like a deep commitment to learning.

Hope jumps off my overfull bookshelves with titles by debut authors.

Hope is embodied in my children as they grow beauteous in their own skins.

Hope has an audacity to it.

Hope looks like protest.

Hope feels like revolution.

Safe & Brave Spaces

Much of my time in the united states has been spent either as a learner or educator in higher education spaces. These spaces, I was told, were liberal havens of tolerance & intellectual freedom. Safe spaces are often unsafe for me.

I learned repeatedly at university campuses where I studied & labored that white supremacy thrives there. Under the guise of diversity or inclusion, these institutions of higher learning perpetuate power hierarchies & imbalances. I was taught curricula that centered whiteness as normative. I was expected to teach these so-called classics. I even pursued fields of study like anthropology & sociology only to uncover that they are in fact whiteness studies. To earn a PhD from an elite university, as I did, is to become an expert in whiteness. These spaces of learning claim to be safe for inquiry. The inconsistencies between the claims of higher education & the realities of relentless discrimination & mistreatment of brown and Black folks resulted in academic trauma for me. My speech was not free. My inquiries & utterances led me to be labelled troublesome, difficult, disruptive & even angry. My outspoken activism was unwelcome. When I declined being used as a face of diversity while being silenced in private offices by supervisors, my unbelonging in these not so safe spaces was complete. I found relentless erasures from my peers & colleagues who envied my outspokenness even as they conspired to remove me from their spaces. The condition of my welcome was my complicity. I often wondered why my critical inquiries & decolonial approaches were shunned or resisted. I questioned myself. I lost my sense of self-worth as I wandered through the pitfalls of erasure & fell in the traps of diversity initiatives. I eventually learned to own my own voice & reclaim myself. This shift meant that I rejected the very premises of my conditional presence on college campuses. There are no safe spaces in the Ivory Tower for folks like me.

Cornel West   The whiteness of (university) is *Jim Crow*, new style.

The way forward is treacherous. If I am serious in my desire to decolonize, I must endlessly reckon with what I was taught & what I learned as normative during my time in higher education. I have much to unlearn. The very behaviors I practiced to get by there are survival tactics that become oppressive. Integrity called my name. I forgive my former self for not knowing what I know now.

We need brave spaces to unlearn, relearn & begin again.

Who is my refuge?
How do I feel safe?
Where is my sanctuary?

Fatima Asghar   *My people my people I can't be lost*
When I see you my compass
Is brown & gold & blood

If they come for us, where will we go?

I woke up today to danger on the horizon.
The elections loom & a wave of white supremacy storms the
Capitol.
If they come for us, where would we go?
We would not go to the white neighbors who have not nodded
to us in the four years we lived next door. We eye their newly
placed "Black Lives Matter" signs in the yard, but we would not
dare knock on their door.
Where would we go?
There is no gurudwara nearby, or we would flee there. There
is no Black Church nearby, or else, we would, like baba's
grandfather years ago, also seek refuge there. There are no Black
or brown families nearby, or else we might find them & offer
them solace, too. Grandmommy has passed on or else we would
find our way to her. She rests, we hope in peace, & I wonder if we
could go to her resting place for refuge to offer prayers there. Our
closest friends who are chosen kin are too far away in Raleigh
& Chicago & New York & Gaborone & Paris, too. My son chimes
in that we are our own refuge. We will need to encourage one
another to brave whatever comes.

When they come for us, where will we flee?

Who do I include in my "us"?
What capitalism & patriarchy & whiteness have taught us
about safety is untrue.
We know that our people-brown, Black & gold-are our safety.
Where they live, we ought to be.

It dawns on me one day as I ponder
who signifies safety for my family
that if we live segregated lives
in gentrified spaces,
it is highly unlikely that our sanctuaries are integrated.

———

Jasmin
Kaur
Sahaara Aspirations | ਸਹਾਰਾ

I aspire to lead my life in such a way that I am a soft place
to land for folks who are intimately oppressed by forces of
unbelonging. May we find each other. May we know reciprocity
& mutuality. May we offer each other sahaara & hosla. May we
tell brave truths to each other. May we call each other in for our
bakwaas. May we speak radical healing love into each others'
broken hearts. May we heal collectively. May our existence be a
balm. May our solidarity be rooted in our virsa & extend to all
humanity.

Let us conjure & imagine new worlds & possibilities.

January, 2021:

The Capitol was stormed by white supremacists & folks of all hues exclaimed "this is not america." Meanwhile, for folks on the margins, every day brings new distressing reminders of white supremacist violence.

———

Emotional Processing

I cannot describe my life circumstances in detailed instances with the finesse of essayists I admire. Trauma memories have dissolved. Words often fail me. Therapy might resurrect a few realizations.

There are far too many silences. That which I have not processed or healed cannot yet be spoken.

I write for emotional processing.

I gesture to events & occurrences, spaces & places, wounds & scars, realizations & inquisitions.

My unbelonging is ongoing emotional processing.

January, 2021:

When I name my grief & anger, it frees me up to create room to breathe. Somehow, I carve out coping strategies for survival. By some magic, I do create joy.

———

W.E.B. Du Bois *It is a peculiar sensation, this double consciousness, this sense of always looking at one's self through the eyes of others, of measuring one's soul by the tape of a world that looks on in amused contempt and pity.*

Many of us were taught that rationality
precludes emotionality.
Binary thinking is a feature of our colonized mindsets.
Unlearning binaries
reveals deep truthful insightful realities.

Lighten up?

My bhai makes a joke about the most recent american tragedy
that to him, sitting across the Atlantic, appears comical. I reply
stone-faced that it is not funny to those who have to survive this
kind of thing daily.
He retorts, what happened to your sense of humor? You used to
be funny. Lighten up.

I simply state, america stole it.
Everything seems heavy all the time here.

Moya
Bailey

Hashtag activism

We need to talk about this. Who is talking about this?
Farmers' Protest. Black Lives Matter. Syria. Uyghur genocide.
The fascism & violence escalate.
Our outrage bleeds from our minds to our fingertips to twitter
& beyond.
We must speak up. We must speak out.
But.
Did we pause? Did we process? Did we take time to learn?

Not all of our words add to light or freedom.

Some of what we say & do stems from shame & pressure.
When we bleed our outrage all over each other,
we often do more harm.

Pyarful Languages of liberation | एकता | ऐेकीकरण

What are the pyar languages of those subjected to perpetual
othering, marginalization, discrimination & policing?

Truth.
Reckoning.
Accountability.
Reparations.
Abolition.
Liberation.

Dignity.
Humanity.
Humility.
Reciprocity.
Community.
Solidarity.

Affirmations for living in america

Black Lives Matter
Black Lives must matter most.
Unless & until Black Lives Matter,
no lives Matter.
Black Liberation is human liberation.
Black humanity is humanity.

Our Black kin remind us time & time again that their minds,
souls & humanity matter. Do we listen?

———

Toni Cade Bambrara   *Revolution begins with the self, in the self... We'd*
better take the time to fashion revolutionary selves,
revolutionary lives, revolutionary relationships.

Even my emotions are regulated by folks policing my identities.
Do I live in perpetual grief
seeking healing? Unfelt emotions are like swallowed poison.

———

Feel it to heal it

Get over it already.
Move on. Chin up.
Grief does not have a timeline or a deadline.
We are ever in recovery.

We are ever healing
from untold losses
hopes dashed
careers derailed
friends unfriended
truths silenced
possibilities dimmed
dreams dashed
plans unraveled
ideas aborted
paths blocked
loved ones estranged
beloveds dismayed.

Grief ongoing seems never ending.
Shall we maintain our facades
as unfeeling automatons
tread on

march onward
unfelt and unfeeling?

Survival?
Day to day living
requires emotional truthfulness.
This I confess–
life's grief is so real.
Its weight does some of us in.
We might succumb to it.

Grief does not have a deadline or a timeline.
We can't rush our recovery.

We can take all the time we need
to feel.
To heal.

Self, naming feelings of marginalization is not a sign of spiritual weakness. Toxic positivity is not healing.

———

When we decolonize, we value EQ as much, or more than, IQ.

Empathy gap? Is it a knowing gap or a feeling gap or a healing gap?

Freeing our emotions

If systems & structures continue to oppress us, it is also true that there are psychological & emotional wounds we bear. Many of us are deeply traumatized even as we cope & survive. If colonialism persists in the mind & on the consciousness level even as folks all over the world fight for sovereignty over their sacred lands, then decolonization must occur on an emotional & spiritual level, too. What might it feel like to heal?

Spiritual gaslighting

I forgive past me for spiritually gaslighting myself and others into believing that we would surmount these many trials & tribulations with just our spiritual fortitude.

As much as our spiritual beliefs & practices teach us the humanity of all beings, we live in a world deeply ravaged by material oppression. I often remind my faith community that we can not preach world unity or human oneness without doing our part to address the tangible ways folks are harmed & marginalized.

What if the marginalized did not marginalize?

What if we did not bleed our wounds of unbelonging all over each other? What if the wounds & scars we know did not turn into weaponized oppressive behaviors? What if we honored our moral obligation to heal fully?

Ally Henny   Antiracism is not work. Some folks do not have the privilege to clock in & out of survival.

An invocation for Antiracism

Antiracism is a way of life.
It is not a sign in my front yard.
It is not a neat reading list.
It is not a checklist.
It is a practice.
It is a mindset & most of all, a heartset.
I vow to exert constant effort & willingness to grow.
As I commit this ongoing daily work in a world
where systemic & pervasive anti-Black racism
persists.
Heart set. Will not rest.

It is empowering to affirm our existence. I exist. I am.

———

There is irrefutable evidence
that a desi-ish African-ish american-ish exists.
I exist.

*What happens to those of us
who are this
&
that?
& that too?
We can't choose.
We are &
Why choose
one piece of ourselves
over others?*

———

Cornel West **Bear witness**

Those of us dwelling in borderless, boundary-free, diasporic
third spaces are capable of bearing witness to humanity.
We bear witness to the truths to which only we can testify.

Diasporic Me

Have you ever tried to explain
to your mother
in her mother tongue
the word diaspora?
Eh diaspora ki he?
What are the words
in any tongue to convey
that diasporic me
is -ish everything
& indigenous nothing?
How do I say
in my Mother's Tongue
that I do not have the words
to explain this kind
of othering
that means that belonging is always
& everywhere.
Unbelonging?

I, the speaker of many tongues,
do not have words for any of this
to identify that to live in the
margins
wherever I be,
is to be in a place rich
with possibility
where I invent words
& worlds
that may not yet be

to convey that
I no longer seek to belong.

The spaces where we belong do not exist.
We build them with radical love
& revolutionary liberation.

ACTIVE MEDITATIONS

UNBELONGING

Speak Belonging

I do not live belonging.
I speak the languages of belonging.
What is the lexicon of belonging?
It is the language of justice.
I have spoken & written & woven & embroidered
these words into every page of this book.

Who taught me how to live?
Who made it possible for me to thrive?

To be -ish
is to be intersectional
& this is to be tired & hopeful & powerful all at once.
To be -ish
is to be &
never either / or
but ever &&

To be -ish
is to normalize unbelonging.

Intersections

All the intersections in me are tired
I am
a brown desi
considered (South Asian)
though by passport citizenship,
African.

I am not Hindu
raised Bahá'í
presumed Muslim.

I hold extensive educational privilege
with no access to generational wealth
barely paying the bills
despite elite educational training
with debt to prove it.

I am first-generation African-born
immigrant settler to the united states
married to a descendant of the enslaved
who built this land and
parent to multiracial polycultural children.

Even in the communities where I reside
or supposedly belong,
I live on the margins.
I am never the center.

Intersectionality
is as much about identity
as power.

Those of us living in the intersectional margins,
who are rarely the center,
do not hold much power.

Where the intersections are so many,
we could either break open the sections
& become wholly human
or be fractured along these lines.

Let me just confess that
life in this divided world
means that all the intersections in me are tired.

& by some unfathomable means,
I persist.

Herein lies my vulnerability & power.

True knowledge?

I was taught a prayer in my Bahá'í upbringing. I paraphrase:
Make of me a hollow reed through which the pith of self hath
been blown so that I may be a clear channel of divine love unto
others.
I realized when I was young that inspiration & true knowledge
do not originate in human minds. They are divinely sourced.
In many academic spaces, ego takes hold. I have been in that
muddled mindset often. Ego is the pith of self. Is it not?

I often meditate for clarity to reconnect my channels of
inspiration to those invisible sources.

Open heart living

The world might disappoint me.
Those I care for might betray me.
People do break my heart.

Yes, I might be hurt.
Yes, an open heart can be a broken heart.
Yes, I am vulnerable this way.

I choose to be open anyway.
Love and live any way.
Broken hearts see and bleed love everywhere.

I am a work in progress.

Unbelonging is a weighted blanket. It weighs me down with keen awareness of my ghubrahats & heartbreaks. In its coziness, I inhale a sense of collectedness. I inhale the scents of nag champa & sage intermingled with lavender & exhale my distresses.
Unbelonging is a place of comfortable unease.
Unbelonging is a weighty blanket of cozy malaise.
I am embraced by understanding in my unbelonging.

Words Matter.

There are words that disown.
There are words that other.
There are words that are weaponized.

And there are words that offer hope, safety & solidarity.

Martin
Luther
King, Jr.

Maladjusted Humans

The world needs those of us who refuse to adjust to injustice.
Adjusting to capitalist exploitation is not success.
Giving in to misogyny is not survival.
Repeating cycles of oppression is not liberation.
I choose to be maladjusted.

Ancestors' guide

I realized that the more we are in touch with our heritage, the more the ancestors whisper in our hearts the truths that tie us together. I used to teach my students that learning is about activating not just the head, but also our hearts & hands. Eventually, I realized this is a core teaching of Sikhi guiding me through my beji, dwelling deep in my core.
Seva. Tan. Man. Dhan. | सेवा | तन मन धन

Human | بشر | इंसान | Humaine

I am 100% human
striving to be humane
seeking to cultivate humanity.

Will this ever be enough?
When will this be enough?
Where on earth will this be enough?

Unbelonging is Solidarity

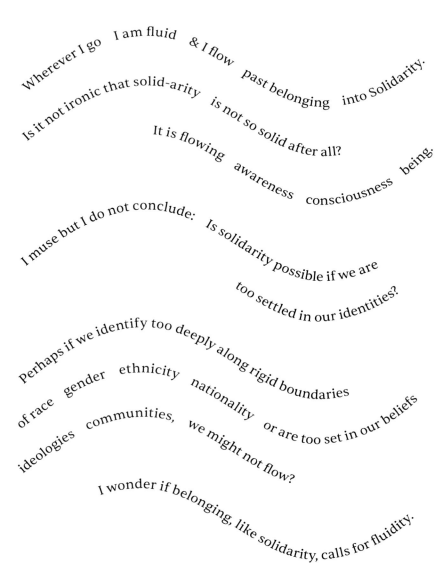

Wherever I go   I am fluid   & I flow   past belonging   into Solidarity.

Is it not ironic that solid-arity   is not so solid after all?

It is flowing   awareness   consciousness   being.

I muse but I do not conclude: Is solidarity possible if we are

too settled in our identities?

Perhaps if we identify too deeply along rigid boundaries

of race   gender   ethnicity   nationality   or are too set in our beliefs

ideologies   communities,   we might not flow?

I wonder if belonging, like solidarity, calls for fluidity.

Mantra for remembering

Remember
your life is a slippery dance.
You may trip and fall.
There are systemic traps
and personal triggers
that leave you feeling less than.
Try not to make space within
for feeling less than.

A love note to the marginalized

We are not alone.
those of us who are -ish
or rarely fit in
or exist only on the margins
when survival mode reigns
& joy is so very rare,
maybe we do not belong anywhere.

Maybe home is not a place.
Maybe our trauma wounds bleed too often.

May we find comfort in knowing that we are not alone.
May we find people who embrace us.
May we be met with understanding & validation.
May we know what sanctuary feels like.
May we imagine, dream, & conjure our liberation.

Here is our mantra:
We Got Us.

Dua for humanity | صلى

May other humans grant me the grace & acceptance I grant them.
May there be space & place for us all to be humanly human.

Prayer for enoughness

oh divine life sources,
remove the shadows of doubt from my heart.
make of me a shining lamp and brilliant star.

Baha'i
Writings

Dua for integrity | دعا

May my life be a testimony.
May integrity guide me
to be vigilant in ensuring that
my thoughts, words & deeds
align truthfully & truly.

May I think liberating thoughts,
feel freeing feelings
& work actively to ensure collective well-being.
May the values & beliefs from my heritage guide
me to soulful authenticity.

May my life be a testimony.

What have I gleaned from this book?
What does unbelonging mean to me?

APPENDIX

Create Your Own Dictionary or Glossary

Words and meanings found and researched:

Words known by experience:

Works Cited

@CornelWest (Cornel West). "To be human you must bear witness to justice. Justice is what love looks like in public -- to be human is to love and be loved." Twitter, 30 Sept. 2011, 3:07 p.m. https://twitter.com/cornelwest/status/119850835986481152?lang=en

Adichie, Chimamanda Ngozi. "The danger of a single story." TED: Ideas Worth Spreading, July 2009, www.ted.com/talks/chimamanda_ngozi_adichie_the_danger_of_a_single_story.

Ahmed, Sara. Living a feminist life. Duke University Press, 2017.

Angelou, Maya. "Dr. Maya Angelou on the Power of Words | Oprah's Master Class | Oprah Winfrey Network." Recorded on OWN, May 28, 2014. YouTube video, 1:07. www.youtube.com/watch?v=BKv65MdlV-c&ab_channel=OWN

Asghar, Fatima. "If They Should Come For Us." 1978. Poetry Foundation, www.poetryfoundation.org/poetrymagazine/poems/92374/if-they-should-come-for-us.

Bailey, Moya. "Misogynoir Nearly Killed Meghan Markle." Bitch Media, 10 Mar. 2021, www.bitchmedia.org/article/meghan-markle-oprah-winfrey-misogynoir.

Bambara, Toni Cade. The Black Woman: an Anthology. Washington Square, 2005.

Brown, Austin Channing. I'm Still Here: Black Dignity in a World Made for Whiteness. Convergent Books, 2018.

Butler, Octavia E. Parable of the Talents. Seven Stories Press, 1998.

Combahee River Collective. "A Black Feminist Statement." Capitalist Patriarchy and the Case for Social Feminism, edited by Zillah R. Eisenstein, Monthly Review Press, 1978.

Crenshaw, Kimberlé. "Demarginalizing the Intersection of Race and Sex: A Black Feminist Critique of Antidiscrimination Doctrine, Feminist Theory and Antiracist Politics." University of Chicago Legal Forum, Iss. 1, Article 8. 1989.

Du Bois, W. E. B. The Souls of Black Folk: Essays and Sketches. A. G. McClurg, 1903. Johnson Reprint Corp, 1968.

Du Bois, W.E.B. "Criteria of Negro Art." The Crisis, Vol. 32, Oct. 1926, pp. 297.

Fanon, Frantz. The Wretched of the Earth. Grove/Atlantic, Inc., 2007.

Fanon, Frantz and Charles L. Markmann. Black Skin, White Masks. Grove Press, Inc., 1967.

Foronda, Cynthia, et al. "Cultural Humility: A Concept Analysis." Journal of Transcultural Nursing, vol. 27, no. 3, May 2016, pp. 210-217, doi:10.1177/1043659615592677.

Freire, Paulo. Pedagogy of the Oppressed. Continuum Press, 1970.

Henny, Ally. Antiracism is not work, Facebook 2 Mar. 2021, 11:20 p.m., https://www.facebook.com/allyhennypage/.

hooks, bell. All About Love: New Visions. William Morrow, 2000.

hooks, bell. "Choosing the Margin as a Space of Radical Openness." Framework: The Journal of Cinema and Media, no. 36, 1989, pp. 15-23.

Jackson, Jesse. "Keep Hope Alive." Democratic National Convention, 19 July 1988, Omni Coliseum, Atlanta, GA. americanradioworks.publicradio.org/features/blackspeech/jjackson.html

Jackson, Sarah J., et al. #HashtagActivism: Networks of Race and Gender Justice. The MIT Press, 2020.

Jaleel, Muzamil. "Poetry in commotion." The Guardian, 29 July 2002, www.theguardian.com/world/2002/jul/29/kashmir.india.

Kaur, Jasmin. If I Tell You the Truth. Harper, 2021.

King, Martin Luther Jr. "I Am Proud to Be Maladjusted." 18 Dec. 1963, Western Michigan University, Kalamazoo, MI.

Lewinsky, Monica. "Roxane Gay on How to Write Trauma." Vanity Fair, 18 Feb. 2021,

Lorde, Audre. Sister Outsider: Essays and Speeches. Crossing Press, 1984.

Love, Bettina. "How Schools Are 'Spirit Murdering' Black and Brown Students." Opinion, Education Week, 23 May 2019, www.edweek.org/leadership/opinion-how-schools-are-spirit-murdering-black-and-brown-students/2019/05.

Love, Bettina. We Want to Do More Than Survive: Abolitionist Teaching and the Pursuit of Educational Freedom. Beacon Press, 2019.

McWhorter, John. "The Dehumanizing Condescension of White Fragility." The Atlantic, 15 July 2020, www.theatlantic.com/ideas/archive/2020/07/dehumanizing-condescension-white-fragility/614146/.

Mock, Janet. Redefining Realness: My Path to Womanhood, Identity, Love & So Much More. Atria Books, 2014.

Mohanty, Chandra. "Under Western Eyes: Feminist Scholarship and Colonial 4tg5y67
≥/Discourses." Feminist Review, vol. 30, no. 1, Nov. 1988, pp. 61–88, doi:10.1057/fr.1988.42.

Moraga, Cherríe and Gloria Anzaldúa. This Bridge Called My Back: Writings by Radical Women of Color. SUNY Press, 2015.

Morrison, Toni. The Origin of Others. Harvard University Press, 2017.

Moyazb. "More on the Origin of Misogynoir." Moyazb. 27 Apr. 2014. moyazb.tumblr.com/post/84048113369/more-on-the-origin-of-misogynoir.

Mpamira-Kaguri, Tabitha. "Trauma not Transformed is Trauma Transferred: What Baton are you passing on?" TED: Ideas Worth Spreading, Nov. 2019, www.ted.com/talks/tabitha_mpamira_kaguri_trauma_not_transformed_is_trauma_transferred_what_baton_are_you_passing_on.

Pierpont, Claudia Roth. "Another Country." The New Yorker, 9 Feb. 2009, www.newyorker.com/magazine/2009/02/09/another-country

Prashad, Vijay. The Karma of Brown Folk. Univ. of Minnesota Press, 2007.

Ricketts, Rachel. Do Better: Spiritual Activism for Fighting and Healing from White Supremacy. Atria Books, 2021.

Slaughter, Danielle. "All The Supremacists Are White, All of The Patriarchy Are Men, But You're Probably A Gatekeeper." Mamademics, 7 Dec. 2018, mamademics.com/supremacists-white-patriarchy-men-youre-gatekeeper/.

Thiong'o, Ngũgĩ wa. "Secure the Base, Decolonise the Mind." 2 Mar. 2017, Great Hall, University of the Witwatersrand, Johannesburg. Guest lecture.

Thiong'o, Ngũgĩ wa. Decolonising the Mind: the Politics of Language in African Literature. James Currey, 1986.

Wood, J. Luke, and Frank Harris. "Racelighting: A Prevalent Version of Gaslighting Facing People of Color." Diverse, 12 Feb. 2021, diverseeducation.com/article/205210/.

Yancy, George. "Cornel West: The Whiteness of Harvard and Wall Street Is 'Jim Crow, New Style.'" Truthout, https://truthout.org/articles/cornel-west-the-whiteness-of-harvard-and-wall-street-is-jim-crow-new-style/.

"The Powerful Lesson Maya Angelou Taught Oprah." Oprah.com, OWN, 2011, www.oprah.com/oprahs-lifeclass/the-powerful-lesson-maya-angelou-taught-oprah-video.

CITATIONS

People Whose Words, Scholarship & Wisdom Inform this Book

Adrienne Maree Brown
Ally Henny
Arundhati Roy
Audre Lorde
Austin Channing Brown
bell hooks
Bettina Love
Brittney Cooper
Chandra Mohanty
Ebony Thomas
Frantz Fanon
Gloria Anzaldúa
Gloria Ladson-Billings
Ibram X. Kendi
James Baldwin
Kimberlé Crenshaw
Kimberly Latrice Jones
Mia Birdsong
Moya Bailey
Ngugi wa Thiong'o
Paolo Freire

Patrisse Cullors
Rachel Ricketts
Sara Ahmed
Tiffany Jewell

Writers of Poetry & Justice who inspire me

Alok Vaid-Menon
Elizabeth Acevedo
Fatima Ashghar
Jasmin Kaur
Leslé Honoré
Mahogany L. Browne
Nayyirah Waheed
Nikita Gill
Rupi Kaur
Safia Elhillo
Shailja Patel
Zetta Elliott

Create Your Own Reading List

Imagine a List of Actions and Activisms

Gratitudes and Acknowledgements

I am beyond grateful to all the folks who have read my words and encouraged me to write this book. Because of you all, I am braver.

I thank all the folks at Mango and Marigold Press, especially Sailaja Joshi, for believing in this unconventional book and for ushering it into publication. Mitali Desai is a heaven sent editor whose thoughtfulness and care with each word made my manuscript a book. Annika Sarin and Divya Seshadri added creative magic to this project.

Were it not for the infinite ways my beloved and life partner, Charles C. Earl, Jr., shows up in support of my endeavors, this book dream would have been deferred indefinitely.

Due to the profound encouragement given by Camille Collins, Dan Moore, Sr., and Kimberly L. Jones, I dared to embark on this daunting venture from writing to publishing. I am humbled by the knowledge that not all who write are published.

This collection exists because the editors at Brown Girl Magazine and South Asian Today published early versions of a few of these verses and reflections. They gifted me with the confidence that comes from tangible evidence that readers exist who might find my words meaningful.

I thank the people who read early drafts and offered enthusiastic feedback: Camille Collins, Tamar Douthit, Mojdeh Stoakley, Jamila Surpris, Dilpreet Kaur-Taggar, Poma Bhowmik, Esmé Rodehaver, Barnali Das Khuntia, Nastacia Pereira, Abigail Biles, Simran Kaur-Colbert, Jumana Master, Mahnoor Khan, Leila Chreiteh, Liz Dwyer, and Erica Dotson. Ciarra Jones, Carol Grady Mansour, and Danielle Slaughter are friends whose clarity when writing about racism influences my thinking. I have been blessed with many brilliant students who became my teachers. I am fortunate to have cultivated a desi writing community. I have learned much about writing, craft, and publishing from supportive colleagues like Jasmin Kaur, Anjali Enjeti, Soniah Kamal, Pooja Makhijani, Aisha Saeed, Sona Charaipotra and members of the Desi KidLit Community.

I felt deeply guided by the ancestors and kin in the unseen realms in my writing journey. Among them, I am most connected with my maternal grandmother who passed away in 1947, her mother, my pa, Sidheshwar Sethi, godmother Alice Williams, and mother-in-law, Joyce G. Earl. I wish they were here to behold this book, co-created by their efforts. My fierce ma, Pratima Sethi, will hopefully read this book as proof of how the perseverance (himmat) she taught me thrives. My bhai, Vishvas Q. Sethi, is one of my lifelong supporters. I owe a huge debt of gratitude to my chosen family all over the world.

I nod to the critics and naysayers. The ones who showed me unbelonging also fueled my resistance.

I am inspired by the ones who call me mama, bibi, aunty, and sister. It is my hope for and faith in them that inspired this offering of community love.

Some verses were previously published in

South Asian Today
Dissident Voice
Brown Girl Magazine
The Aerogram